BLESSED ARE THE WHOLLY BROKEN

by
Melinda Clayton

BLESSED ARE THE WHOLLY BROKEN

by Melinda Clayton
Copyright 2013 Melinda Clayton

This book is a work of fiction. While some of the place names are real, characters and incidents are the product of the author's imagination and are used fictitiously. Any resemblance to events or persons living or dead is purely coincidental.

ISBN 13: 978-0-9963884-4-3

ISBN-10: 0-9963884-4-3

Library of Congress Control Number: 2016903349
Thomas-Jacob Publishing, LLC Deltona, Florida

First Printing: October 2013
Second Printing: March 2016

Published by Thomas-Jacob Publishing, LLC
Deltona, Florida
USA

Dedication

To my family, with love and gratitude.

Acknowledgments

Many thanks to my legal expert, David K. Bowles of Bowles Lutzer & Newman, LLP, as well as to my medical expert, Jennifer Bunn, RN and co-author of the textbook *Microbiology Fundamentals: A Clinical Approach*. To both of you, your time and expertise were invaluable; any mistakes are solely my own.

I'd also like to thank the staff from the Lauderdale County Jail in Ripley, Tennessee, who were friendly and helpful during phone calls asking about procedures and processes. Again, any mistakes are mine.

Thanks, too, to my beta-readers and editors. Your careful attention to detail made all the difference.

Blessed are those who mourn, for they shall be comforted.
Matthew 5:4

Prologue
Ripley, Tennessee
May 13, 2013: Sentencing

Around me I hear the sounds of incarceration echoing against cold concrete: shouting, banging, an occasional sob. The air is putrid, a stale mixture of urine, sweat, bleach, and vomit. In the beginning I could scarcely fathom becoming used to such things, but after nearly a year in this cell, in some odd way the noise and the stench have come to represent home. I'm comforted by the consistency of the assault on my senses, much as one finds comfort in the numbing monotony of white noise.

The call came exactly four minutes ago, so I wait for the armed guards and the quick trip to the courthouse where I will meet my attorney. Together, we will face the jury—a jury of my peers, they said, and at one time that would have been accurate. But these people are no peers of mine; I've crossed a line that ensures this to be true.

There is no doubt of my guilt; that was already determined. What is in dispute is the depth of my guilt. For weeks I sat at the defense table, my mouth dry, my eyes drier, and listened to the horror of my crime. The carefully prepared defense of my actions crumbled away like so much dust in the wind, blown apart by my own behavior. By the end, even I knew I was a monster, not for the reasons they cited—not because I had killed my wife—but because I didn't save her sooner.

More recent words play themselves through my mind as I wait for the telltale jingle of keys. *Aggravating factors. Particularly cruel, stood to gain sole custody of a minor, planned and premeditated, preyed upon vulnerabilities.*

It is not enough to label me guilty; the question is: Am I guilty enough to put to death?

It is a necessary part of the process; this, I understand. The court needs closure, the jury needs to feel they've fulfilled their responsibilities, the family needs to feel vindicated. True and just punishment must be meted out within the appropriate parameters of the law.

I will go with my lawyer into the courtroom. I will sit again, as I have sat for weeks, and wait for others to determine my fate. Life imprisonment or death; that is the question. And while the outcome matters immensely to the other players in this drama of my life, it matters not at all to me. I am dead either way.

Chapter 1
Memphis, Tennessee
February 14, 1989

When I think about the day I met my wife, what I hear is rain. It coursed down the dorm room window in great rivulets that February of 1989, pouring from the sky in quantities sufficient to ensure the students splashing along the flooded campus on the way to class would be soaked to the bone in spite of their shiny raincoats and colorful umbrellas.

On that particular day, the fortuitous rainy Valentine's Day that would set the future course of my life, I stood on the tenth floor of Richardson Towers South, listening to the rain drum on the roof and staring gloomily out the window. I was a conscientious student; rarely did I miss a class. But that winter morning of my senior year at Memphis State University—later renamed University of Memphis—I couldn't bring myself to slog to the far corner of campus for a microbiology lab I disliked even on the sunniest of days.

"Damn rain," I muttered, and heard my slumbering roommate stirring on the other side of the desk that served to separate our room into halves.

"Again?" He sat up, scrubbing his face in an attempt to wake up. "Jesus, will it ever stop?"

Brian and I had been roommates since sophomore year, one of those rare pairings that worked effortlessly from the beginning. Ironically, given the differences in our personalities, it was odd we ever even met. Brian Stone was an athlete, a former football player, whereas I got winded merely anticipating the long trek downstairs during one of our many late night fire drills. He began his time at MSU housed in South Hall, the athletic dorm, where he stayed until his disdain for curfew, coupled with his love of girls and beer, resulted in his removal from the team. I returned from summer break to find Brian's smelly duffel bags tossed onto the bed I had come to think of as my own.

Despite our differences, our personalities and temperaments were such that even after semesters spent tripping over each other in our cramped and crowded dorm room, we remained friends. Brian's easygoing nature and innate optimism took the edge off my own anxiety-driven self-doubts, and I don't think it's too much of a stretch to believe I helped Brian find his footing at MSU. The Brian of our senior year was a much more focused young man than the Brian who had his filthy feet propped on my desk—*my* desk—that first day of our sophomore year.

"Yes, again," I answered him, leaning my forehead against the cold glass of the window, fogging it with my breath. "I'm skipping class."

"You?" Brian threw off the covers and padded over to peer out the narrow window with me, rubbing the stubble along his jaw. "Now *me* skipping class, that's pretty much a given, but *you*? Phillip Lewinsky doesn't skip class. And it's only Tuesday," he pointed out. "Not a great way to start out your week."

"I'm tired of being wet," I said, "and cold. It took forever last night for my feet to unshrivel."

Brian yawned loudly, scratching at his belly above the sagging sweatpants he wore as pajamas. "Looks like a good day to skip out on everything," he said, as I leaned away from him, waving my hand against an invisible cloud of morning breath.

"You smell like something crawled inside and died," I informed him, and he laughed.

"Not all of us are as hygienically scrupulous as you," he retorted. Brian had a way with words, a deep appreciation for vocabulary; this was a fact that often seemed incongruous with the rest of his personality, though it served him well in the years to come.

"Hygienically scrupulous?" I repeated. "Who says that? No one says that, Brian. Seriously."

He gave me a sideways look. "Well of course they don't," he said. "That's what makes me special. Just as not everyone flosses three times a day, deep conditions once a week, and trims nails on Sunday." He poked a finger at my chest. "That's what makes *you* special."

Against my will, I felt myself blush, a trait I hated about myself. "I'm not that bad," I said, though in truth I probably was. Living in such a confined space didn't leave much room for secrets. "It just seems a little overboard because you're so nasty in comparison. How many showers did you take last week? Two? Three, at most?"

Brian snorted. "Not all of my showers are taken here, you know. I have …" He paused, face squinted in apparent concentration as he searched for the right term. "Friends. Yes, that's it. Friends of the female persuasion who enjoy sharing shower time with me." He grinned again. "How do you think I keep these golden locks so irresistible?"

It was true, both the boastful claim and the golden locks. Girls did tend to find Brian irresistible. Although he hadn't played football since freshman year, he was obsessive about his workout routine. The end result was that aside from his love of advanced verbiage, he still presented as a football player. Brian's looks may have helped reel the girls in, but it was his temperament that kept them there. My own mother was smitten with him. "Such a charming young man," she always said, and make no mistake, Brian knew just how to capitalize on his natural gifts.

Men liked Brian, too. What wasn't to like? He was a man's man, as my father said. I knew exactly what my father meant, because I knew in my father's opinion, I wasn't. My father and I didn't have a contentious relationship; we were cordial with one another. But my father and Brian were never at a loss for words on any number of topics, from sports to cars to rabbit hunting.

I used to watch them as they talked, the way my father's eyes lit up. I wish I could have been the one to do that for my father, but I wasn't, and after years of trying, and failing, to connect, I'd ultimately given up, content to bask in the residual glow of his enjoyment of Brian. I might not have been able to live up to my father's expectations, but at least I'd given him Brian; I learned to enjoy my father's pride vicariously.

In hindsight, I think they each filled a need for the other. Brian was the son my father had hoped to have, and my father filled the void left by the man who abandoned Brian a month before he was born. Brian rarely talked about his childhood, and I didn't press the issue, but if talking with my father about his desire for Memphis State to return to the Final Four helped him in some way, I was happy for him.

His family relationships may have been rocky, but Brian's success with the ladies of MSU was legendary. It was virtually guaranteed on nights I returned late from the lab I'd find a piece of tape placed over the keyhole, my sign to knock and then retreat to the study lounge down the hall while Brian roused himself enough to escort whichever coed he'd been entertaining down to the lobby for checkout. Brian was a scoundrel, no doubt, but he was a likable scoundrel, the only person I've ever met who somehow managed—and still does—to maintain friendships with women even after breakups.

I, on the other hand, was apparently quite easy to resist. It wasn't that girls didn't like me, per se; it was more that they didn't notice me. Slightly built with dark hair that was already receding in spite of the weekly deep conditioning so adroitly noted by Brian, I was overly serious and had a tendency towards moodiness, a tendency the incessant rain wasn't helping. The only consolation I had was that the rain might at least keep people indoors so I wouldn't have to witness happy couples parading around campus with flowers and candy while I spent Valentine's Day exactly the way I'd spent it the previous twenty-one years: alone.

"Come on, Lewinsky," Brian said, delivering a soft punch to my bicep. "Let's go get some breakfast. This room is depressing."

Brian threw on a t-shirt and flip-flops, and we headed downstairs to the cafeteria that connected Richardson Towers South with Richardson Towers North, the girls' side of the dormitories. During the years I called the university home, the Towers were the closest thing to coed dorms MSU had. They may still be; I haven't visited the campus since shortly after my graduation.

That dreary morning the cafeteria was nearly deserted, which is part of the reason Anna was impossible to miss. But only part. The real reason Anna couldn't be missed was that she entered the room on her backside, with a tremendous crash of table, chairs, books, and papers.

It was, she later told me, one of the most embarrassing moments of her life, slipping in a puddle of rainwater just as she strode through the door. "But only one; I've had several," she admitted. "I'm a little clumsy." I loved her clumsiness almost as much as I loved her candor.

But that was later. I had no way of knowing as Brian and I jumped to help her collect her belongings, trying our best not to laugh, that this was the woman I would one day swear to honor and cherish until parted by death. And I certainly hadn't known I would be the one to part us by death, or that Brian would be left alone fighting to allow me a life I no longer wanted.

Chapter 2
Ripley, Tennessee
June 3, 2012: The arrest

"I came as soon as I got your message." Brian's voice was ragged as he set his briefcase on the scarred table that separated us and impatiently waved away the guard. I remained silent as he pulled out a chair and dropped into it, running his hands through hair that was still golden, if shot through with a generous amount of silver. He looked at me, eyes narrowed in an unspoken question, as if waiting for me to clear up a terrible misunderstanding. "Phillip? What's going on?"

I said nothing as he continued to stare at me. When the young officer had read me my rights and I had said that yes, I did want an attorney, I'd been thinking of Brian not as an attorney, but as a friend. I hadn't been thinking of legal representation at that time. It was indisputable that I had killed my wife; there were at least four witnesses who saw what happened, and besides, I wasn't disputing it. I had held my son close and waited quietly for law enforcement to arrive. On their order, I had handed Peter to one of the officers and placed my hands behind my back, surrendering to arrest without incident.

To their credit, aside from "Watch your head," and "Through this door," the officers hadn't said another word to me, waiting, I suppose, until my attorney could be present. I also remained quiet, not out of any fear of having what I said used against me, but because I simply had nothing to say. I had no thought of trials and juries and pleas at that time. I had just lost my wife and had my child ripped from my arms. At that moment, I wanted my friend.

Across from me Brian shoved back his chair, the legs screeching across the worn floor, and stood, hands on hips, pacing in front of me. "You need to tell me what's going on, Phil." His distress was palpable; I could feel it in the air between us, in the clipped way he said my name.

I shrugged, raising my hands before dropping them into my lap, at a loss for words. I suppose it's likely I was in shock, but I was ignorant of the symptoms. The intake nurse had signed off on her paperwork without comment, and given what had landed me in that hard chair in that cold room, further medical assessment probably wasn't at the top of the state's agenda at that moment.

"Damn it, Phil." For a man who loved words, Brian seemed as at a loss as I, and possibly in shock, as well. "Damn, damn, damn," he punctuated each word with a slap to the table and then sat again, leaning towards me in disbelief. "They're saying you killed Anna."

I struggled to answer him, to bridge the disconnect between brain and body, willing my lips to open and my tongue to move. "I had to, Brian." The words were thick, slurred. Across from me, I heard his sharp intake of breath.

"My God," he said. "It's true?" He pulled away from me so quickly he nearly overturned his chair. "You *had* to? What does that even mean, Phillip?" He stood again, hands pressed to either side of his head as if to block out the words, and resumed his pacing, unable to be still.

My mouth seemed full of paste, refusing to co-operate. It was impossible to believe just a few short hours ago I'd been singing lullabies to my son.

My son. "Where—?" I swallowed against the dryness in my throat and tried again. "Where's Peter?"

Brian turned, staring at me. "You don't know?" Underneath the anger, I could hear a catch in his voice. "Le Bonheur, Phil. Airlifted." He blew out a breath. "It's touch and go. They're saying you did that, too." His voice cracked. "Please tell me you didn't hurt Peter."

Fear and anger sliced through the fog surrounding me and I sat up straight. "How could you even ask that?" As crazy as it may seem, regardless of the reason for my incarceration, I couldn't believe Brian would ask me such a question. "Brian, I would never … Oh, my God, my little boy." Once acknowledged, the pain was overwhelming. I felt as if my insides were curling in on themselves, shrinking into a white-hot ball of pain.

"They're trying to reach Anna's family as the next of kin," he said, then sat down again, seemingly hit by a new realization. "Anna's family," he repeated, and shook his head as if to clear it. "Their world just blew up and they don't even know it yet. What happened, Phil?" The anger in his voice had faded to an ambiguous grief. "Tell me what happened."

Brian had been my friend for a quarter of a century and Anna's for nearly as long. It wasn't that I didn't want to tell Brian what had happened, but that words literally failed me; I didn't know where to begin. Where is the beginning of any story? How does one point to any specific event and say, "There! That's where it all began."

Brian wanted to know what had happened *that* day. How had Anna and I gone from a loving couple on the eve of our twenty-third anniversary, to this? But it didn't begin on that day. I supposed it all began on that rainy day in 1989 when Anna came sliding into the cafeteria of Richardson Towers, bowling over not only a table and chairs, but me—and Brian—as well. So that's where I began.

Chapter 3
Memphis, Tennessee
February, 1989

She was a senior, Anna was, on the day that was later determined to be Memphis' rainiest day in 1989. She was also skipping class, after having had her umbrella blown inside-out by the cold winter wind. Once we'd picked her up and helped her gather her books and papers, we'd managed to talk her into joining us for breakfast despite her embarrassment.

"What I really wanted to do was run to my room and cry," she told me later, "but you guys wouldn't let me escape."

She was right; both of us had urged her to join us. I was immediately smitten, in my awkward way, nearly too shy to speak, while Brian was as smooth as ever, bringing her coffee and wiping crumbs from her chair before she sat. Though he would later argue with this, I suspect he initially viewed Anna as he viewed all women: as a potential conquest.

Anna accused him of this many years later, on one of our frequent camping trips into the Smokies.

"Not true," Brian said, as we sat around a bonfire in the mountains outside of Gatlinburg, drinking beer and tossing logs onto the fire. "I love all women, but Anna, I especially loved you. Still do." He tipped the neck of his beer bottle towards her in a silent toast.

From across the fire Anna had smiled at him, I remember, as she always smiled when he made those pronouncements, but her eyes had shone with a hint of sadness in the flickering light of the flames. In the rare cases in which Brian was unable to coax a woman to fall in love with him, he was still able to trigger some sort of maternal response. Anna loved Brian, too, but Anna was *in* love with me. This, I never doubted, at least not back then. Nonetheless, he called forth within her some sort of protective instinct. Anna saw a measure of loneliness in Brian that tugged at her heartstrings, more so as the years passed by.

"All the women," she had once told me shortly after our wedding, "are just a cover." She unclipped her hair and shook it over her shoulders before climbing in and settling herself against the pillows of our first bed, rubbing lotion between her palms to warm it before smoothing it vigorously along her legs. I watched her, as captivated as always, and leaned over to plant a kiss on her bare shoulder. The softness of her skin never failed to amaze me.

"Think about it, Phillip," she continued, oblivious to my advances. "He came from a troubled family with a drug-addicted mother. He's still searching for her. Emotionally, I mean." I watched as she smoothed the lotion into her calf in quick, circular motions, loving the sound of her voice while simultaneously wanting her to hush.

"It's why he goes from woman to woman but never stays with any of them. He loves women," she said, screwing the cap back on the lotion and massaging the last traces into her hands. "I really believe he means it when he says that. But he never trusts that they love him back. It's sad, isn't it?"

"Who cares?" I had answered, tugging her against me, impatient with her analysis. "Enough about Brian. What about me? I'm searching for love, too." She had laughed then, and I feel confident in saying neither of us spared a thought for Brian the rest of the night.

It's possible, even likely, Anna was right, but as a young man who'd spent more time as a third wheel than as a partner, it was difficult for me to muster sympathy for Brian's self-inflicted game of musical women. Anna was different, though. She had a knack for seeing inside a situation and understanding each of the separate composite parts that made up the whole. I suppose this was why she chose philosophy as her major, a fact that led to no end of teasing from Brian.

"What good is a philosophy degree?" he asked her several weeks after our first meeting. We were sitting on the side of a planter in the courtyard of MSU (even now, I refuse to say UofM), enjoying the warm spring sun between classes, and I recall being transfixed by the play of light on the auburn of Anna's hair. I wanted to fall into that hair, I remember, wrapping myself in the wildness of it. Brian must have felt the same, because he reached over to tug at a curl as he asked the question.

"How about it, Socrates? What does one do with a degree in philosophy?" he asked again, with a grin.

"Find someone who'll pay you to sit on a mountain and think?"

She took the teasing in stride, as she took most everything in her own quiet way. Anna always exuded a Zen-like peacefulness that, during our marriage, was one of the things I loved most about her. Since her death, however, it has become one of the things I hate. But I'm getting ahead of myself again.

I suppose it may seem odd to outsiders that the three of us spoke so openly about our affection for one another, particularly the affection Brian had for Anna, but that was the foundation of our friendship. We were unabashedly honest with one another, but I've come to wonder what good it does to be honest if the other person doesn't understand the honesty for what it is. This is the question that haunts me.

Anna and I were a solid couple by that spring, a situation I still can't quite believe. I think we'd both felt it from that very first meeting; I know I certainly had. To say we clicked fails to describe the depth of the connection we felt. It was more as if we recognized each other, had even been expecting each other. *Oh, there you are*, I remember thinking as I grasped her hand to pull her from the puddle on the floor. *I wondered when you'd come.*

For once Brian was the odd man out, and I suspect our sudden role reversal felt as strange to him as it did to me. To his credit, he handled Anna's gentle rebuffs with grace, and I do believe he was happy for me. Brian was, first and foremost, my friend.

I wonder now how things might have turned out differently had she chosen him instead of me. I've no doubt he wonders the same

Chapter 4
Memphis, Tennessee
February, 1989

"You're so serious," Anna had told me on our first date. "An old soul."

"Not always," I found myself feeling defensive. "I know how to have fun, too." A jolt of alarm went through me. Was she saying I was boring? Was this the dreaded friendship speech I'd heard all my life? In the few short days I'd known Anna, I'd become hopelessly infatuated, amazed that she seemed drawn to me, too. As I mulled over her words, my heart began to sink.

We were walking along the cobblestones, watching the barges stretched out along the Mississippi River. The sun was setting, framing Anna's silhouette against a fiery backdrop, and as her curls blew about in the breeze off the river, I remember thinking of Aphrodite, both beautiful and terrifying, and wholly mesmerizing. I was lost.

In the distance stylish couples boarded a riverboat for an evening cruise; laughter floated back to us on the breeze. Farther down, a group of teenagers listened to a boom box, the bass a steady vibration in my chest. The rain had finally moved on, the air carrying a hint of the spring to come, but the evening was still chilly. I put my hand on Anna's back, gently steering her back toward the car, which I'd parked just off of Riverside Drive.

We'd spent the afternoon strolling around downtown Memphis, listening to blues bands busking in the park. Some of them were quite good, young people close to our age clearly on their way up, while others were older, the years etched into their faces, crashing back to earth after whatever small measure of fame they'd managed to claim had begun to seep away. The juxtaposition of the two ends of the spectrum was sobering, to say the least.

I was keenly aware in those days that wandering too far into the night could be dangerous. Memphis is a beautiful city in many ways, rich with history and music, but a devastating poverty seethes just beneath the surface, and the accompanying resentments are never far away. Although the evening appeared peaceful, I was eager to get Anna safely back to campus before the last rays of sun disappeared. Given her most recent statement, I was also searching for a way to complete my mission without drawing attention to my motives. To be labeled *serious* at the age of twenty-one was bad enough; I didn't want to also be labeled a worrywart. She might be rejecting me, but I'd protect her until the end.

Luckily, she followed my lead without question, apparently too intent on our conversation to notice I'd quickened my pace. "Of course you're fun; that's not what I meant," she was saying. "Maybe *serious* is the wrong word. How about earnest? What I'm trying to say is that you're real, Phillip. I like it."

In the beginning, Anna always called me Phillip. I'm not sure when she stopped, resorting to the natural shortening of my name. I know I didn't notice it until after Jeffrey died, when the act of speaking that extra syllable—when saying anything at all—seemed to require more energy than she could muster. As silly as it may sound, particularly given all we'd suffered at that point, it saddened me, as if I'd slipped a notch in her esteem, no longer worthy of those extra letters.

But that balmy night in 1989 we were as yet untouched by tragedy; we had no way of knowing what fates awaited us, and I was beginning to feel the stirrings of hope. The night was young, the air was crisp, we had the world before us, and maybe—just maybe—she wasn't rejecting me, after all.

I opened the door for her, ever the gentleman, torn between asking her to explain what she meant, and enjoying what she'd said without testing my luck. As I settled myself beside her and adjusted the mirrors, she made the decision for me.

"You're different, Phillip," she said, turning sideways in her seat to look at me, and my heart stuttered from the closeness of her. I could smell her shampoo, and I remember vividly how I'd longed to push her hair back from her face, anything just to touch it.

She continued, oblivious to my angst. "You're not like other guys. Like Brian." That caught my attention, since I'd harbored a secret fear he'd steal her away from me. "I mean, I like Brian," she said, "but he doesn't let people get close enough to see who he really is. With you, I feel like I know you. Like I've always known you." She smiled, tentatively at first, and I leaned over to kiss her, one quick little peck before I lost my nerve.

For a moment we just sat and grinned at each other, until I finally came to my senses and engaged the ignition. I was beside myself with happiness, thrilled to drive down Poplar Avenue holding her soft hand within my damp one. This was a gesture that would become as comfortable to us as the old MSU t-shirt Anna wore to bed long after our graduation. Always, as we drove—crossing nearly all of the 48 continental states at some point during our marriage—I held her hand across the seat.

This was true even on the day I killed her.

Chapter 5
Memphis, Tennessee
May, 1989

Aside from his rough start at MSU, Brian was overall a good student; he was set to graduate on time with us, with a respectable grade point average and a bachelor's degree in criminal justice. The three of us celebrated together with a spirited weekend on Beale Street before settling down to take a more serious look at our futures. I no longer remember whose idea it was to rent an apartment together, but shortly after graduation the three of us found ourselves sharing a two bedroom in a seedy area of Midtown.

Things were different in those days, at least as far as our families were concerned. I'd have no more shared a room with Anna than I'd have gone streaking through Midtown in broad daylight. That isn't to say we were completely innocent of one another. By that time, we'd moved past quick kisses and begun a barely restrained exploration of each other among the cracked vinyl seats of my old car. But to have openly shared a room would have displayed a tawdriness out of place in our relationship. What we had was special, and we agreed, without even speaking of it, to keep our relationship pure—with the occasional exception of those stolen moments of passion in my backseat. Instead, for the short time Brian lived with us he and I shared a room, something we were used to doing, after all, while Anna bedded alone. Even so, our parents had been none too pleased with the arrangement.

"It's not right," Anna's father told us when we met with her parents over dinner to tell them of our plans.

It was the week before graduation, and Brian was with us; Anna's father had insisted on meeting him, too. "He wants to make sure I'm not moving in with any bad elements," Anna had explained, causing Brian to laugh.

We had arranged to meet downtown at the Rendezvous, and I was quickly coming to second-guess the wisdom of that decision. It's hard to make a good impression when one is covered in barbecue rub. Across from me, Mr. Tyler continued to voice his concerns, presumably unaware of the spices that clung to his chin and threatened at each breath to break free and take refuge in my glass of tea. It was difficult not to stare.

"It's not that I don't trust you boys; it really isn't. You seem like nice kids, and Anna has nothing but good things to say about you." He gestured wildly towards Anna as he spoke, and I quietly moved my tea glass to the other side. "She's a smart girl; I have to trust her judgment, right? But what will it look like to people, my daughter moving in with two young men? What'll I tell people who ask?" The chunk of spices finally broke free, landing—to my great relief—somewhere on his lap.

"How will we explain it to Cathy?" Anna's mother interjected, plucking anxiously at the buttons of her blouse. She was a small woman, quiet and unassuming, and nearly invisible next to the mountain that was Anna's father. "Anna, she looks up to you, you know."

Cathy was Anna's younger sister and from the stories Anna had told me, worrying about the impact our shared apartment would have on Cathy should have been the least of Mr. and Mrs. Tyler's concerns. According to Anna, who gave me a warning pinch under the table, nineteen-year-old Cathy had already discovered that anything you could do in a shared apartment you could also do in a dorm room, a parked car, or on a park bench, for that matter. But it certainly wasn't my place to share that with Anna's parents.

In the end it was Brian who charmed his way past their concerns. "We'll take good care of Anna," he assured Mr. Tyler. "A young woman shouldn't be alone in a big city like Memphis. She'll be safe with the two of us; we'll make sure of it."

Mr. Tyler gave a receptive nod. "You make a good point," he said. "I reckon if she's dead set on living in the city, and it looks like she is, she could do worse than to have a couple of young men for protection."

Brian's presence wasn't required at the meeting with my parents, but he tagged along anyway. I was glad for his company; he had a way of smoothing the rough edges of my family. "What are you worried about, Phillip?" he asked, noticing my hesitation when we pulled into the drive of their Bartlett home the following night. "What's the worst they can do? You're a grown man."

"It's not what they might do," I told him, opening Anna's door and helping her out. "It's what they might say. I never know what's going to come out of my dad's mouth."

My mother, while not as verbal with her concerns, made her feelings known through a series of sighs and worried glances as we gathered around the table. That evening, instead of ribs my mother served up lasagna, a dish with just as much potential for mishap, causing me to wonder briefly why the biggest events of our lives tend to be discussed over food and the embarrassing complications it can present. I handed Anna an extra napkin as she struggled with a stubborn string of melted cheese, then turned towards my father as he spoke.

"Don't you go getting this girl pregnant, Phil," he said, and I felt Anna startle beside me, while across from me Brian snorted, unable to hide his laughter. My father continued, oblivious. "I know you say you two aren't sharing a room, but I was a young man once, too, and I know how these things go. Keep it wrapped up. You hear what I'm saying?" He tore off a bite of garlic bread for punctuation, regarding me from under bushy brows as he chewed.

"Daniel," my mother interjected. "Was that really necessary?"

"What? You're too easy on the boy, Maria. Brian knows, don't you Brian? You know what I'm talking about. Boy better keep his pants zipped."

I would have given anything at that moment to melt away into the linoleum, my embarrassment was so acute. Even worse, I had the distinct impression that underneath the rude warning he was in some way proud of me, hoping, maybe, I'd finally be a *normal* young man, the kind he'd expected when the doctor had announced with a flourish, "It's a boy!"

Later, on the short drive back to the dorm, I tried to apologize. "He can be an ass sometimes," I said, but Anna dismissed the topic with a wave of her hand.

"I think he's kind of cute," she said. "In a rough sort of way."

"Your dad's okay, Phillip," said Brian from the back seat. "He's just trying to look out for you." He broke into laughter again, unable to contain himself. "Keep it zipped—oh, my God, that's priceless." By the time we reached the dorm, all three of us were laughing, my embarrassment forgotten.

With the difficult task of announcing our plans to our parents completed, we were on our way, all three of us, and excited to be there. Brian had done well enough on the state test to land an entry-level position as a probation officer with the juvenile justice system. While I was initially surprised at the career he decided to pursue, in retrospect, it made perfect sense. Brian knew as well as anyone the hurdles faced by children caught up in the system.

That was the thing about Brian. On the surface, he was a playboy, the stereotypical jock. But those of us who knew him understood his philandering approach to life was carefully crafted to hide a sensitivity of startling depth. This would never be more evident than in the months following my arrest, though we could not have imagined, as we unpacked our meager belongings in the shabby little apartment, the heartache awaiting us years down the road.

Anna, having realized there was some small truth in Brian's teasing, had a more difficult time with job hunting. Within a few weeks of graduation she decided to apply to graduate school. "There seems to be a hiring freeze for the position of sage," she told Brian, smiling. "Not enough room on the mountain. For now I guess I'll have to keep my deep thoughts to myself while I pour coffee and bus tables."

As for me, I'd landed a job as a lab technician for one of the hospitals downtown. The hours were long and the pay wasn't great, but I felt like the luckiest guy in the world. First job, first apartment, first girlfriend, best friend. What more could I have possibly wanted?

When I remember that year it's as if I'm straddling a line between then, and now, fully a part of each reality while at the same time separate from it. In many ways, we remained true to our younger selves throughout the years. If one only sees the surface of our lives, we look like any other group of adults, hitting milestones, fulfilling expectations.

Anna and I married, as everyone had assumed we would, and I began the long process of moving up the career ladder, eventually becoming the director of a medical lab in the city of Dyersburg. Anna completed her graduate degree and climbed through the levels of her own career, ultimately becoming the Dean of Students at a community college close to my office.

To our great surprise Brian also found his way back to school, obtaining a law degree from the University of Tennessee and ultimately building a successful law practice not far from our old apartment. He was a more polished, more accomplished Brian with an even larger vocabulary, but he was still Brian.

He had dozens of friends and even more women. He had an income that was more than adequate to provide not only the necessities, but many of the finer things in life.

Throughout our marriage, Brian remained a steady fixture; it's impossible to remember us, Anna and me, without also remembering Brian. He met us out for dinner and drinks, spent holidays with us, and even kept a change of clothes in the closet of our guest room. He accompanied us on many of our hiking and camping trips, as avid a lover of the outdoors as was Anna. On some occasions, if the weather was particularly chilly or the water especially rough, he and Anna braved the wilds without me as I, less adventurous than they, relaxed at the campsite, catching up on reading or cataloguing plant species, content to greet them with a warm fire and a cold drink on their return.

I was never jealous of their friendship, and I never doubted their loyalties. Some would call me a fool for my blind trust, but I believed in the bonds we had; I never had reason not to. If anything, at the end of it all, it was I who failed them.

Aside from a brief—and nearly forgettable—marriage in his late twenties, Brian remained ever and always the same incorrigible bachelor he'd been in our college days. If we came over time to view him as the *puer aeternus*, our own eternal boy, he willingly accepted the role.

We provided him family and stability, a port in the storm, and he provided us an indirect experience of freedom and spontaneity. He crash-landed among us with some frequency, and while we privately lamented his seeming inability to settle down, some small part of me—and I think of Anna, too—ultimately came to envy the autonomy with which he lived.

Brian had all the trappings of a successful life, but he didn't have what Anna and I had, that spiritual connection that comes from spending years building a life with someone you love. Perhaps I should have pitied him for that—Anna always had—but I didn't, not then. After all, Anna and I came to know what it felt like to have our world ripped apart. We knew what it felt like to bear the unbearable, to have loved and lost. Brian had never loved in such a way; therefore, he had never lost in such a way. This was what I had believed, and I had envied him.

But I was stupid.

Chapter 6
Memphis, Tennessee
September, 1989

Our wedding was small and simple, held on a warm September day in 1989 in the Tyler family's rose garden. It was an intimate gathering of close friends and family; we shunned anything larger. We were of the age that both of us, together and apart, had suffered through our share of weddings. The summer after our graduation it seemed nearly everyone we knew was getting married, and it was after one incredibly long and complicated—and undoubtedly expensive—ceremony that I hoped Anna was sufficiently sentimental to consider accepting my proposal.

I had managed to scrimp and save enough over the summer to buy her a modest diamond. The jeweler had assured me it was of the best quality, but it was nowhere near the size of the rings many of her friends were sporting, and this worried me a bit. I had carried it in my pocket for days, waiting for the right time and place while also working up the courage I needed to go through with it.

It was sometime during the lighting of the candle at that long and complicated ceremony that I determined this would be the day I proposed to Anna. Once the decision was made I could hardly sit through the rest of the ceremony without fidgeting. The room suddenly seemed too small, the crowd oppressive. My tie was choking me, and sweat dripped between my shoulder blades as I waited through what seemed an endless prayer. When the songs were finally sung and the groom had kissed his bride, I turned to Anna to suggest we leave, only to find her lifting the hair off her neck, her face flushed.

"Let's get out of here," she said. "This is all just too much." I smiled, flooded with feeling for this woman whose thoughts were so much my own. I led her by the hand through the crowd, bypassing the receiving line and ducking through a side door, finally emerging into a narrow alley shaded with elms.

"Thank God," we said at the same time, and then laughed.

I shrugged off my coat and yanked my tie loose. "Was it just me," I asked, leaning against the building, "or did that seem to go on forever?" I glanced over at Anna, did a doubletake.

"Forever," she agreed, bending down to step out of the pantyhose she'd somehow managed to push down to her feet without me noticing. She struggled to remove a foot, tripping in the stretchy material, and I reached over to steady her. "Thank you," she said, laughing at the expression on my face. "Well, it's hot, isn't it? And I hate these things. The slip is next, so if that's going to embarrass you, you might want to turn around."

Sometime during the final prayer I had determined to take Anna to the riverfront to propose. It seemed fitting, after all, since that was where we'd had our first date. But as she stood in front of me shoeless, her feet tangled in the discarded pantyhose, I was suddenly on one knee without remembering precisely how I'd gotten there. Her eyes grew huge as she realized what I was doing.

I fumbled with the box and felt my cheeks flaming. "It's not much," I said, and cursed myself for saying it. "I mean, I wish I could—" I stopped again. *Stupid*, I told myself. *Why don't you just point out how broke you are? That'll make her say yes.* I looked up at Anna to see her smiling down at me, and my breathing returned to normal.

"Anna," I took her hand. "I'm trying—not very well—to ask you to marry me. So, how about it? Will you?" I hated how desperate I sounded, but in truth, I was.

She bent down and kissed me on top of the head. "I would love to marry you, Phillip," she said, stroking a finger down my cheek. "But only if you promise our wedding won't be like that one. That was a little over the top for me. And if you'll help me out of these awful stockings before someone sees us."

We decided on September, and Anna wore ivory, not one of those full, flowing dresses most brides seem to prefer, but a soft, clingy gown that fell just above her ankles and hugged her curves in all the right places. She carried a bouquet of late-blooming roses from the garden, and she was beautiful. I get a lump in my throat just remembering.

Brian was my best man, and Anna's sister Cathy was maid of honor. I had met Cathy a handful of times by then, and I'd never known quite what to make of her. To label her flirty would be an understatement. She found occasions to rub against me, lingering too long when I hugged her in greeting, leaning in too close when we fixed our plates at family dinners, bending over in front of me when she seated herself across the table, affording me a generous view of her even more generous cleavage.

At first I thought I was imagining things. After all, until Anna no girls had ever even noticed me, and I knew if it weren't for Anna, Cathy and I would have never crossed paths. Young women like Cathy weren't interested in young men like me. I knew this from years of ruminating on the unfairness of life.

Cathy was a beautiful girl, in an overstated sort of way; I remember thinking of her as an exaggerated version of Anna. She had Anna's delicate features but emphasized the exotic tilt of her eyes—a feature of Anna's I adored—with dark, heavy makeup. Her lips were slightly fuller than Anna's and thickly glossed, and her figure was curvier, straining against the tight tank tops she seemed to prefer.

Although I favored Anna's natural beauty to Cathy's more flamboyant style, I had no doubt Cathy had her pick of young men, and I initially chastised myself for reading more into her actions than was surely warranted. Cathy was just more exuberant than Anna, I told myself, and I, as a relatively inexperienced young man, was overreacting. Before long, however, I couldn't deny her flirtations were intentional.

Over the weeks of our engagement I had managed to ignore Cathy's unwanted touches and insinuations, diligently side-stepping her embraces and avoiding conversation, but then she upped the ante, leaving me no choice but to respond. It happened the week before our wedding, as Anna and her mother sat at the kitchen table and made plans, and I, tiring of the sitcom Mr. Tyler was watching and in need of fresh air, made my way to the back hallway in search of the garden. Just as I reached for the doorknob, I felt a hand slip into the back pocket of my jeans and cup my hip. I turned, startled. Anna would never have touched me in such an intimate way in her parents' home. But Cathy, it turned out, would.

As I spun to face her she kept the original offending hand in my pocket and encircled my waist, pressing her pelvis against my groin as she slipped her other hand into my remaining pocket. There I was, in a full-on frontal embrace with my soon-to-be sister-in-law, shocked speechless as she pressed into me, groping my behind.

"Cathy," I managed to sputter as I gripped her elbows, attempting to pull her arms away from me. "What are you doing?"

She tilted her head back to look into my face, and laughed. She looked so much like Anna, but wasn't Anna at all. "Relax." she said. "Take a chill pill. I'm just giving my new brother a hug." With a final squeeze she released her hold on my hips and stepped away, disappearing into a nearby doorway so quickly I almost couldn't believe it had actually happened.

I worried over the incident for at least a week before I decided to talk with Anna. I had no idea how she'd react, but I felt I needed to be honest about what had happened. I also dreaded my next visit to her parents' house. I was marrying Anna, for heaven's sake. I couldn't spend the rest of my life in fear of being groped by her sister. I had to tell her, and I finally worked up the courage the next Saturday morning as we strolled through Overton Square, sipping on carryout coffee and enjoying the morning.

She listened without commenting, walking quietly beside me with her hands wrapped tightly around the Styrofoam cup. When I finished she sighed, her mouth a grim line. "I'm so sorry, Phillip." She looked up at me, but I couldn't read her expression through the dark lenses of her sunglasses. "Cathy is a mess; she always has been," she continued. "I don't know why, but she's always seemed to feel as if we're in competition with each other. Maybe because I'm the oldest? Who knows," she answered herself.

"My friends, my accomplishments, my boyfriends, it didn't matter," she said. "Whatever I had, Cathy wanted. And the thing is"—she ran a hand through her hair, her voice rising, clearly frustrated—"it's not as if she really cared about any of it. Whether it was a blouse, a pair of shoes, or a person, she only wanted what I had so I wouldn't have it." She looked up at me again. "Does that make sense?"

I nodded; I understood what she was saying, but the implication gave me pause. "The things that make you happy," I said, searching for words, "the people—she doesn't want them for their value to her; she wants them because they have value to you."

Anna nodded. "And she wants to take that away from me."

I put my arm around her, and she leaned against me as we walked. "But why?" I asked, knowing Anna had no answer. "I always wanted a brother, or a sister, someone to share my childhood with. I'd have given anything to have a brother a couple of years older than I am. Like a built in best friend. I can't understand why she'd want to hurt you."

Anna shrugged. "My parents have gone through hell with her," she said. "We all have. She's always been angry, not just with me, but with everyone. My mother tells stories about Cathy's tantrums as if telling the story somehow makes it humorous, as if it were just one of those terrible twos things that parents have to deal with. But it wasn't like that at all. It was scary. And they don't know the half of it."

I was left to wonder how far Cathy had gone—how far she would go—to hurt Anna. The thought was unsettling.

I hadn't returned to the Tyler's home until the rehearsal the evening before our wedding, and I was nervous about seeing Cathy again. As it turned out she was perfectly cordial, as if nothing had ever happened. I'm sure it helped that Brian was with me. At any rate, I was relieved, and I hoped Cathy and I could bury the past and move forward without further incident. I was naïve back then. I had no inkling of the dark forces that drove Cathy's behaviors. I doubt Cathy herself knew what motivated her to act as she did.

The rehearsal was the first time Brian and Cathy had met, although I had told him about my own odd encounter with her. In true Brian style, he had laughed. "You're getting married," he said, jabbing me in the chest, "but I'm not." He grinned. "I can't wait to meet her. Is she hot?"

As if a kindred spirit, temperature was also Cathy's first thought. "Who's your hot friend, Phil?" She was sitting on the back steps in a tank top and shorts, legs splayed as she painted her toenails, when we walked up the path for rehearsal.

Before I could reply, Brian stepped in. "I'm Brian," he said with a wink and a smile. "And I'm single." I left them to each other and went in search of Anna.

I found her at the kitchen table with her mother, patiently removing the thorns from a stack of roses. "To carry tomorrow," Anna said, tilting her face towards me. "Aren't they gorgeous?"

"Not as gorgeous as you," I said, leaning down for a kiss, surprising both of us with my boldness. Although we'd been dating over six months, I was notoriously shy about showing affection in front of Anna's parents. But she had looked so cute sitting there, cross-legged in the kitchen chair surrounded by flowers, I couldn't resist.

"It's okay, Phil," her mother said, smiling. "You can kiss her now, but not for too long." She shook a finger at me, and I laughed aloud, surprised by her comment. "It's good to have you join our family," she said, reaching out to pat my hand, and I was suddenly struck by how similar to Anna she was. An older version, to be sure, but with the same sweetness and sense of humor.

As awful as it sounds, I'd hardly paid attention to Anna's mother. She always seemed to stand in the shadows of her family, alternately worrying over Cathy or reassuring her husband. Mrs. Tyler was a quiet woman, and I wondered sometimes if she'd always been quiet, or if she'd simply given up trying to be heard after the many years she'd lived with Anna's rebellious sister and apprehensive father. I was oddly pleased, if slightly embarrassed, to be at the receiving end of her teasing, and I found myself wanting to get to know her better.

The rehearsal went off without a hitch, save the fact Brian and Cathy didn't show up until it was over. I didn't ask where they'd been; I didn't need to. Neither did Anna or her parents. I wondered if they were as relieved as I was at Cathy's absence.

The wedding the next day unfolded exactly as Anna and I had wanted. Surrounded by those closest to us, we pledged our love and stepped together into our future. We were young and idealistic, as most young married couples are. We saw the future as a long, vibrant road of endless possibilities. Perhaps the harshest lesson of all is that nothing is endless.

Chapter 7
Ripley, Tennessee
June 3, 2012: The arrest

"I can't be your attorney," Brian said, startling me from my memories. He was pacing again, holding a hand palm-out as if to stop my words.

"I hadn't expected you to," I said. "You're here as my friend, Brian. They asked if I wanted an attorney and I said your name. That's when they let me place the call."

Brian nodded slowly, as if in thought. "Then how do you plan to explain at the arraignment that you don't have an attorney?"

I hardly knew what an arraignment was, and said so to Brian.

"You'll go before the magistrate," he said, "maybe tomorrow, but more likely Monday. You'll be told the charges and asked if you want an attorney. You do, but it can't be me, so don't even suggest it. I'll try to come up with some names for you. They'll ask how you plead, but you don't, not until you have an attorney. If it comes up, we should both say that this initial consultation was covered by the attorney-client privilege, so neither of us will have to divulge anything we said to each other, but after that, you need new counsel. And they won't consider bail, Phillip. Not under these circumstances."

That got my attention. "I have to have bail, Brian. I have to get to Peter."

Abruptly, his pacing stopped. "Phillip," he said, bending towards me, hands on his hips. "You don't get it, do you?" He spoke slowly, as if to give me time to process the words. "Peter's *gone*." His voice was harsh. "They think you tried to kill him. You won't be allowed any contact with Peter."

I sat back, momentarily stunned into silence. "But I didn't," I finally managed to say. "I would never, ever hurt Peter. They'll see that, right? And then I can see him?"

Brian hesitated. "If it comes out during the trial that you aren't responsible for Peter's injuries, child welfare will take that into consideration. But Phil, there are so many factors in question. You'll also be charged with the murder of … of Anna." He paused again, and I saw his throat working as he struggled to maintain control. "I can't possibly predict the outcome of all this, Phil. And even if I could …"

"What? Tell me, Brian." My heart was pounding under the thin material of the county's jumpsuit.

"Even if I could," he said, turning his back to me, "it may be too late for Peter."

"What do you mean? What are you saying?"

But he didn't answer me; he simply paced.

Chapter 8
Memphis, Tennessee
June, 1995

"I want a baby," Anna said, apropos of nothing. We were packing, preparing to move to Ripley, Tennessee. In some ways it was difficult to leave the little apartment we had at one time shared with Brian, but it was time.

Anna had finished her graduate degree a couple of years prior, and although she'd accepted a job teaching in the city school system, her ultimate goal was to teach at the college level. There were aspects of her job she enjoyed, but it was also challenging, offering few resources to the impoverished kids with whom she worked. She was restless, ready to move on, so when I was offered a midlevel job with a medical lab in Dyersburg, our decision didn't require much thought.

"What did you say?" I thought I must have misheard her. We'd discussed having children, of course, and I was certainly open to the idea. I just hadn't expected to hear that from Anna that summer afternoon of 1995. Always before, when we'd discussed starting a family, we'd decided the time wasn't quite right.

"You heard me," she said, smiling. "I want a baby." Her hair was pulled into a ponytail, the loose strands curling around her face in the humidity. She was barefoot, dressed in cut-off denim shorts and a white sleeveless blouse, and I could think of nothing I'd rather be doing than giving her a baby.

"Like, right now?" I asked, returning the smile. "I'll have to clear these boxes out of the way, but I'll do my best."

She laughed and threw a roll of packing tape in my direction. "Not at this exact moment," she said, "but soon."

I taped a box of books closed and slid it towards the door. "What made you change your mind? Not that I have a problem with having kids; you know that. But why now?"

"Why not now?" she responded. "It's the perfect time. You're getting a nice raise, we're buying our own home out in the country, and I'm leaving a stressful job behind. Everything's falling into place, don't you think?"

I hadn't thought about it until then, so preoccupied was I with the move and all it entailed, but I had to admit she was right. We'd closed on a three-bedroom house that Anna referred to as "adorable" and I referred to as "affordable." It was located on five acres just north of Ripley, within easy driving distance of my job, but rural enough to allow us the privacy we wanted. It was natural to complete the picture by adding a couple of kids, a swing set, maybe a dog.

"Then let's do it," I said. "Let's have a baby." I was rewarded by a lapful of Anna as she leapt across the boxes to give me a kiss, which I happily received.

"Unless you want to start this project now," I said, laughing as she pushed me down, "you'd probably better get off my lap."

"Now is fine," she replied, and our packing was finished for the day.

Chapter 9
Ripley, Tennessee
October, 1997

The first question any couple is asked after marry-ing is, "When are you going to have a baby?" Although frequently annoyed by it, Anna and I had gotten used to deflecting that question in the early years of our marriage. She was still in school, I was building a career, and we had a small apartment in the middle of Memphis. The reasons for waiting were plentiful and easily understood.

Not so after years of trying. At that point, the questions were no longer annoying; they were painful. We didn't worry at first. We were healthy adults, in so far as we knew, with a normal sex life. If it was meant to happen, it would. We told ourselves this for two years, years during which we made Ripley our home. We settled easily into our new house. We joined a church and made new friends. We took pleasure in painting and papering and landscaping. I tilled a sec-tion in the back, and Anna planted a small garden. We had squash and tomatoes, turnip greens, lettuce, and radishes.

We even harvested a couple of pumpkin plants, and while our yield was small and sickly due to the late planting, we spoke easily and often of the joy we'd eventually experience with our children. I envisioned the planting, small hands dropping the seeds, and the hoeing, as I instructed on the proper technique. Anna, I knew, dreamt of jack-o-lanterns and trick-or-treaters, costume parties and shrieks of laughter.

And so it was on a beautiful fall day in 1997, as Anna scooped pumpkin seeds into a colander to be washed, that she finally brought up the topic both of us had surely been thinking. "We need to see a doctor, Phillip."

I didn't ask why, because I knew the answer. Our attempts to have a baby had morphed from a healthy enjoyment of our sex life to calendars, thermometers, and a slew of drugstore pregnancy tests, all negative in the end. We'd gone from daydreaming out loud all the scenarios our baby would complete, to tense silences, both of us afraid to speak the words.

"Two years isn't that long, Anna," I said. I wasn't sure why I was balking at the thought of medical intervention. Maybe it was because to give in to it would indicate some sort of failure on our part. It stung that we couldn't seem to achieve this most basic of human functions.

"I'm thirty years old, Phillip. We're not kids anymore." She turned off the faucet and stared out the window, avoiding my eyes. "How long should we wait? Until I'm thirty-five? Forty?"

I stepped behind her to encircle her waist, pulling her against me. She leaned back, tilting her head to look up at me. "When I was a little girl," she said, "I wanted to marry a wonderful man who'd love me forever."

I leaned down to kiss her on the nose. "You did," I said, "and I will."

She gave me a sad smile. "I know." She patted my cheek. "But I also wanted to have a houseful of kids. I know two years isn't that long, but I feel like I'm running out of time. You work in a medical lab, Phillip. You know the challenges older women face. What's the magic age? Thirty-five? That's not that far away. Maybe nothing's wrong, but if something is, I need to know it so we can fix it. Don't you agree?"

I did agree, but even if I hadn't, I would have done anything for Anna.

Chapter 10
Ripley, Tennessee
June 3, 2012: The arrest

"Why are you telling me this, Phillip?" Brian had finally given up pacing and stood with his back to me, hands shoved deep into his pockets.

"I need you to know," I said.

"To know what? How hard you and Anna worked at having a baby? I do know that, Phil. I stayed with you for days after Jeffrey was born, remember? And again for Peter."

This was true; Brian had visited with us both times Anna had given birth. He'd been the godfather of both of our children. He'd also been there when we'd lost Jeffrey, and for many days after. I don't know how either of us could have survived without him. Not only had he held Anna as she cried, he'd been the one person who understood what I needed, even when I didn't know it myself. He let me rage when I needed to rage, and be silent when I needed to be silent.

Finally, ever so gently, he had nudged each of us, kicking and screaming, back into the world, and he'd anchored us there ever since. Brian knew so much about us, but he didn't know everything.

"But you weren't there before," I said. "You didn't see how hard it all was on Anna."

Brian spun around to face me. "So I took a couple of years off to have a life of my own, and that's somehow a problem? That has something to do with all this? Jesus, Phillip." He was angry partly, I think, because I wasn't explaining myself well, but partly because given the enormity of my circumstances, he didn't know how else to react.

I shook my head, desperate to make him understand. "No, Brian. No, that's not what I meant. I'm sorry; that came out wrong. I just meant I need you to know what that whole experience did to Anna—to us. There were things we didn't share, times we found it easier not to talk about. I need to tell you about those times. Then you'll understand."

"I wouldn't bet on it," Brian said, and turned back to face the wall.

Chapter 11
October, 1999

Neither of us, as it turned out, had any detectable medical reason for having failed to make a baby. No low sperm count, no endometriosis, no hormonal imbalances. When all the tests were completed and all the results were read, we were sent home and told, essentially, "Relax and have sex. It'll happen."

While on the one hand we were both relieved to know there were no issues with our plumbing, so to speak, that still didn't answer the only truly important question we had: Why, then, can't we make a baby?

"Maybe they're right," Anna said one night as we sat in silence, she with a book in her lap and I catching up on some lab notes I'd allowed to fall behind. "Maybe we do just need to relax and stop worrying about it. I mean, if all the parts are working right, it stands to follow at some point it'll happen. Or we'll grow old trying. Worrying about it isn't going to change the outcome, at least not in any positive way."

I looked up at her, taking a moment to pull my brain away from cell morphology and blood types to focus on what she'd said. "Look, Anna," I said. "I've been thinking. We'll have a baby, one way or another. We can always check into artificial insemination, or in vitro, or whatever the hell it is. Or adoption. I'm open to adopting, too. We'll do whatever we need to do. Right?"

I was rewarded with a smile the likes of which I hadn't seen for months. Anna's whole face curved when she smiled; it was impossible not to smile back. She unfolded herself from the couch and came to sit in my lap. "Are you seriously willing to check into those things?" she asked.

"I am," I told her. "Of course I am."

She wound her arms around my neck and pressed her cheek against my chest. "That's such a relief to me, Phillip. Thank you."

I stroked her hair, remembering how I'd spent months longing to lose myself in those curls back when we were college kids. It was on the tip of my tongue to suggest we give the natural method of impregnation another go when I realized Anna was asleep, heavy against my chest, her breath warm and steady on my neck. I gathered her to me, like a precious gift I didn't want to lose.

"I think I'm coming down with something," she said the next morning. I'd managed to rouse her enough the previous night to get her to bed; she hadn't even bothered to put on a gown. Instead, she'd stripped out of her clothes and pulled the covers to her chin, asleep before I'd closed the door. I hadn't joined her until the wee hours of the morning, after completing the reports I'd brought home and swearing—not for the first time—not to allow myself to fall so far behind again. She hadn't stirred when I'd stripped off my own clothes and scooted next to her in search of warmth.

I looked up from the newspaper that morning, vaguely anxious. Anna was the healthiest person I knew, seldom ever sick. She ran two miles each morning and was an avid biker, hiker, and camper. Vacations for us typically meant either a campsite or a cabin; no trendy Las Vegas trips or Carnival cruises for us. But that morning she did look pale, and her coffee sat in front of her untouched.

I reached across the breakfast bar to feel her forehead. "No fever," I pronounced, but you look tired, hon. Why don't you call in sick today and get some rest?"

"I think I will," she said, surprising me. Anna had never taken a sick day. She stood and came around the bar. "Bye, sweetie," she stood on tip-toe to kiss me. "I'm going back to bed."

"Call me if you need something," I said. "This isn't like you."

"I'm sure it's nothing a day of rest won't fix."

"I could always take a day off, too," I said. "Keep you company. Work on this baby thing."

She smiled. "I appreciate the offer, but I believe I'll take a rain check. I'm not sure your definition of 'rest' and mine are the same." She kissed me again before padding down the hallway and gently closing the bedroom door.

She wasn't sick, of course, and after a week of exhaustion during which she barely managed to keep any food down, and then only the blandest of offerings, our suspicions were confirmed: After all the years of trying, the stick was finally blue.

"I've never been so excited to feel so sick," Anna said, beaming up at me from where she lay on the couch, an afghan drawn up to her chin. Her face was pale, emphasizing the dark circles under her eyes, but she'd never looked more beautiful to me. I pulled her feet into my lap and began to massage them, pressing my thumb in a circle over the ball of her foot. Anna sighed contentedly and snuggled further into the cushions.

"Who should we tell next?" she asked, her voice already fading into sleep. She had called both sets of parents right away, but other than that, we'd not made any official announcements.

"Brian?" I suggested. Truthfully, I was happy to have an excuse to call him. It had been close to two years since we'd seen him, the longest we'd ever gone, and our last visit had been a surprisingly uncomfortable encounter. It had been the first, and last, time we'd met his wife.

Brian had surprised everyone by getting married, not only because none of our old crowd had known he was seriously dating anyone, but also because they had eloped. None of us had known a thing about it until Brian began working his way down a list of phone calls in the winter of '96. Anna had been the one to answer the call; I'd been on the porch replacing a rotted slat in the swing.

I knew immediately it was Brian; I could tell by Anna's pleased tone. This was in the middle of our attempted baby-making years, and while Anna hadn't yet reached the level of anxiety she later attained, hearing her voice raised with pleasure was a welcome circumstance.

I'd just stepped inside when Anna came running into the room, motioning me to pick up the corded extension on the mantle. "Brian?" she was saying. "I'm going to have Phillip get on the extension so you can tell both of us about it, okay?"

I picked up the phone just in time to hear Brian's voice, sounding unusually hearty. "Get him on here, too, Anna," he was saying. "I want to introduce both of you to Sylvie."

I raised my brows at Anna as she mouthed, "His wife."

I nearly dropped the phone.

"Phillip? You there, Phil?"

"Brian!" I finally managed. "What's up, man? Anna came running in here as if you had something important to tell us." I shrugged in Anna's direction. What else was I supposed to say?

"I did it, man." He laughed into my ear. "I bit the bullet. I want you to meet Sylvie, my wife."

"Hello?" A sultry sounding voice floated through the lines. "Phillip and Anna? Brian has told me so much about you."

I wish I could say the same, I thought, but managed to keep from saying. "Sylvie!" I had said, sounding like an idiot. "Well, this is a nice surprise. Brian?" I stumbled; I had no idea what to say next. Luckily Anna rescued me.

"Brian, this is so exciting. You'll have to bring her here right away so we can meet her." She shrugged back at me. "Sylvie? What works for you guys? Next weekend? I'll fix a nice dinner and we'll celebrate."

As it turned out, they didn't make it that next weekend, or for many weekends after. It almost seemed as if Brian found excuses to keep us from meeting, so many and varied were the reasons he gave for their inability to visit. It was spring before we finally pinned them down, and even then, they could only spare a couple of hours. Instead of meeting at our house, we made the drive to Memphis, where Brian had purchased a townhome near the Racquet Club shortly after landing a job with one of the oldest law firms in Memphis.

We met at Half Shell, and Anna and I had just been seated when Brian came hurrying in, accompanied by a tall, willowy blonde who looked exactly like someone with whom I would have pictured Brian. Dressed to the nines, lots of jewelry, long nails painted a fire engine red. Beside me I could feel waves of curiosity coming off of Anna. We both wanted to hear when and how they'd met, how long they'd known each other, what their courtship had been like. Unfortunately, we didn't get the answers to any of those questions.

Dinner was rushed, with Brian apologizing profusely, explaining that he was working on a big case and scarcely had time to breathe, much less eat. Anna tried to pull information from Sylvie, but her answers were perfunctory, leaving no room for exploration, and the conversations fell flat. We left the dinner with no more understanding of Sylvie, or her relationship with Brian, than we'd had when we arrived. We'd promised to get together again soon, when there was more time, but it never happened.

I had spoken with Brian occasionally over the following couple of years, but about nothing of substance. He seemed curiously remote and I missed him, we both did, so it was with great anticipation I looked forward to calling him with our good news.

"Call him now," Anna said, rousing enough to exchange feet so I could massage the other one. "I can't wait to let him know he's going to be Uncle Brian." She smiled, and I reached over to the end table for the cordless phone.

"Do you want to talk with him?" I asked, but she shook her head.

"You tell him," she said. "I know you're dying to."

I punched in the numbers and waited, only to be greeted by Brian's prerecorded message on his answering machine. "He's not home," I said to Anna. "Should I leave a message?"

"Just ask him to call us as soon as he can," she said. "I don't want to leave it on a machine."

Anna called Cathy with the news next, but her reaction was harder to read, as it usually was. Although she'd had a string of unhealthy relationships by that time, she'd remained single. Anna and Cathy had never been close, and the separate paths they'd chosen only took them further apart as the years went by. Neither of us was sure how she'd react to news of Anna's pregnancy; as it turned out, she didn't have much of a reaction at all. "Cool," she said. "So what else is new?" And that was that.

With our phone calls complete, we spent a relaxing evening watching rented movies and sharing a bowl of popcorn. Anna napped periodically through the evening and I watched her sleep, profoundly moved by the reality of her carrying our child. After the years of worrying and trying, unsuccessfully, to have a baby, our dream was finally coming true.

Brian didn't return our call that night, or the next one either. By the time he finally reached us, we had nothing to tell him.

Chapter 12
Ripley, Tennessee
June 3, 2012: The arrest

"What are you talking about?" Brian asked, running a hand through his hair. "Jeffrey wasn't born until 2001. Anna couldn't have been pregnant while I was still married to Sylvie."

I said nothing, waiting for Brian to put the pieces together. I knew the precise moment understanding dawned.

"She had a miscarriage," he said, once again lowering himself into the chair across from me.

"Two." I said, and his mouth dropped open. I cleared my throat. "Anna and I have had four children," I said. "Two died in the womb. And Jeffrey," I drew a shaky breath, and Brian, his anger forgotten, reached to put a hand on my shoulder. "And now Peter."

"I had no idea, Phillip." He was silent for a moment before continuing, "That must have been awful, after thinking finally …" He didn't finish the thought. "I was so caught up in Sylvie back then, and our sham of a marriage. I can't believe I wasn't there for you guys through all that. I can't believe I wasn't there for Anna."

"She knew you had to live your own life, Brian. We didn't expect you to come running every time something happened."

"But I always had," he said. "That's why I didn't."

"What do you mean?" I couldn't understand what he was trying to say.

"I mean," he rubbed at a scar on the old wooden table, "I had to put some distance between us. Between you and me, but also between me and Anna."

"Why, Brian? Why would you do that?"

He was up again, pacing. "Because I couldn't stand watching the two of you play house," he said, a sliver of anger returning to his voice. "The two of you belonged together, that was obvious, but that didn't make it any easier to witness. It's not easy, always being the odd man out. I thought if I left, if I settled into my own life, made my own marriage, instead of always intruding into yours ..." He stopped, leaning his forehead against the wall. Behind the glass, a guard moved forward, but Brian waved him away. "It didn't work, of course." He turned to face me. "All it got me was a nasty divorce and a serious dent in my bank account." He smiled a crooked smile. "And a lot of lonely days."

Maybe I had known all those years that Brian's words to Anna, though said in jest, were full of truth. I suppose I had. But I hadn't realized the extent to which he'd had to fight against them, or the extent to which his feelings for Anna had shaped his life. I don't know what I might have felt at that moment had our circumstances been normal. Jealousy? Anger? What I did feel was sorrow, for Brian, for Anna, for all of us.

"We have to take care of Peter," is what I said to him. "I need you to help me get to Peter. He's all that's left of Anna."

Chapter 13
November, 1999

There aren't words in the English language sufficient to describe what Anna and I endured those
next few years. We lost our first baby just after Anna's
second appointment with her doctor. "On the next
visit," the doctor had said, "we'll listen to the heartbeat." We were ecstatic. Anna called both of our
mothers and told them to save the date. Our parents
were as excited as we were, and Anna wanted to include not only her own mother, but mine. It was one
of the many things I loved about Anna, that she so
readily incorporated my mother into our lives. I was
not always as thoughtful; luckily, Anna picked up my
slack.

She called to invite them, but it was I who called
to tell them it was not to be. The first few weeks of
that pregnancy were very difficult for Anna. She was
terribly sick, not just in the mornings but throughout
the day. She was an adjunct professor at that time,
teaching only a handful of classes each week while
hoping to work her way up, and she told me she

made it through each hour with a handful of loose crackers in her skirt pocket and a can of diet soda on the desk.

Even then, she was a trooper. Despite the sickness, despite the exhaustion, it was perhaps the happiest I'd ever seen her. "It'll pass," the doctor assured us at her first appointment when we asked about the symptoms. "Drink plenty of fluids and rest when you can. Come back in a couple of weeks, just to be safe, and we'll see how you're doing."

To the doctor's credit, the nausea had begun to abate by our second appointment. Anna looked much better, her cheeks had some color, and she was holding down food. The doctor gently felt her abdomen and declared all to be well. We had no reason to believe anything would go wrong before we returned at twelve weeks to hear the heartbeat.

It was a Friday night, and isn't it strange how such details embed themselves into our memories? We retired early, Anna because she was tired, and I because I wanted to be with her. We joked about becoming boring, and concluded that was the natural progression for those about to become parents. We talked for a while in the darkness, batting around baby names and discussing the renovations needed to turn the nearest bedroom into a nursery. She asked me to rub her lower back, something she'd often asked, and I did so happily, already loving the changes in her body, determined to be as much a part of the experience as I could. We fell asleep spooning, me behind Anna with my arm around her, holding both of them close.

It was I who awakened. The night was a cool one, but I felt dampness against my thighs. I thought at first Anna must be too warm, sweating in her sleep; we joked that she'd become a living furnace since becoming pregnant. I moved away from her and pushed the comforter aside to cool her off. I squinted at the bedside clock, noted it was just past midnight, and reluctantly swung my legs off the bed and headed for the bathroom, cursing the beer I'd had before turning in.

As strange as it may sound, I didn't immediately understand the meaning of the blood smeared across my crotch and thighs. It shames me to remember it now, but initially I thought it must have come from me; all sorts of ridiculous scenarios flew through my groggy mind until I realized I felt no pain, just the mild discomfort of a full bladder. When I finally comprehended, when I finally understood the source of the blood, I slammed the bathroom door open and literally leapt across the room to Anna, shaking her awake while simultaneously turning on the lamp on her nightstand.

A thousand times over the intervening years, I've wished I could relive that moment. It marked the beginning of a very difficult time for Anna and me; I'm not sure we ever fully recovered. Actually, I'm sure we didn't.

If I could relive that moment, I'd lower myself onto the side of the bathtub and wait. I'd allow her a few more moments of happiness, and when I had to tell her, when I absolutely couldn't wait any longer, I'd kneel in front of her band wake her gently. I'd smooth her hair from her face and kiss her cheeks and wrap my arms around her and tell her I loved her. I'd hold her close and tell her we had our whole lives, we had the whole world, and we had each other; that was all we really needed. But I didn't know, so that's not what I did.

When it was all over, when Anna was back home and her mother was in the kitchen puttering around making soup, I sat on the side of our bed and cried. Anna was sleeping, helped along by a prescription from the doctor. I cried for our baby, and I cried for me, but mostly I cried for Anna.

Later, when her mother had retired to our extra bedroom for the night and I held Anna close, she turned to me. "Phillip," she said. "As awful as this is, as unfair and heartbreaking and terrible as it is, there's something positive about it, too."

I searched out her eyes in the darkness, waiting for her to continue.

"At least I know I can get pregnant, Phillip. If it happened once, it can happen again. At least I know we can."

How I wish I'd told her then that we only needed each other.

Chapter 14
Ripley, Tennessee
June 3, 2012: The arrest

Brian and I sat silently as he digested all I'd told him. He'd been there less than an hour, but it seemed much longer. The guards outside the glass looked bored, and I wondered if the look was affected after so many years dealing with criminals, or if it was genuine. Perhaps, after witnessing countless stories of human tragedy, one becomes immune.

"You're killing me, Phil," he said after some time, and I looked away. He no longer paced; instead, he sat quietly across from me, seemingly resigned to hearing my tale whether he wanted to or not. I had never before seen that look on Brian's face, not even when his marriage ended. I think he may have known then, or at least suspected, what was coming.

I've wondered since my arrest, during the months of my incarceration and through the long days of my trial, if I should have spared him. No doubt it was selfish of me to unburden myself at Brian's expense, but as I've relived these events over the past year, I've come to understand that I was always selfish where Brian was concerned. I hadn't meant to be; I hadn't even realized I was, but in hindsight the truth is inescapable. While Anna and I, or perhaps just I (Anna did, after all, try to understand Brian) smugly defined life as married versus not married, or settled versus not settled, Brian unfalteringly supported me in whatever decision I felt compelled to make at the time. I like to think I supported him, too, but the truth of the matter is he never asked for support, and I was so caught up in my own life I rarely thought to give it.

In my defense, if such a thing exists, I must say that in the beginning, on the day of my arrest, I wanted nothing more than to be free to be with Peter. When I'd placed the call to Brian, I hadn't been calling an attorney; I'd been calling my friend. But I've wondered since then if some part of me, some small part that wasn't shocked numb with grief, knew that Brian could better help me in his professional role. I'd been desperate to tell him our story; I needed him to understand, but was it because I longed for comfort from my friend, or was it because I needed his help in getting to Peter? In the end, the answer didn't matter.

"It kills me, too, Brian," I finally said, because it did, all of it, my shame suffocating me behind the locks and bars.

Chapter 15
Chattanooga, Tennessee
January, 2000

We took a trip to Chattanooga after Christmas, a long weekend to relax and regroup. It was nice to be outside, engaged in physical activity. We took a tour through Ruby Falls, hiked through Rock City, and enjoyed a late picnic lunch of cold chicken, potato salad, and iced tea at the precipice of Lover's Leap. The wind was cold, but the sun was warm on our backs as we took in the view and tried to identify the seven states supposedly visible from the top of Lookout Mountain.

I held Anna's hand as we walked the trails, taking her arm in the most treacherous spots, aware of her tendency to trip over her own feet even without the added danger of rocks and tree roots. I enjoyed this quiet time away with her. In the earlier years of our marriage we'd traveled frequently, but the last few years we'd been so focused on starting a family we'd neglected nearly everything else. We passed several families along the trails, parents cautioning young children as older children ran ahead, and while the thought crossed my mind that that could someday be us, their presence didn't stir up any feelings of sadness at our lost chance. We had time, I told myself.

Anna, too, seemed optimistic about our future. "Thanks for this, Phillip." She gestured at the view as we packed up the remains of our lunch. "This is exactly what we needed. It's beautiful, isn't it?"

"Not as beautiful as you," I told her, a play on an old line. I expected—and received—a good-natured eye roll at the cheesiness of the compliment. I was serious, though. Anna looked beautiful, well-rested and fit, her cheeks pink from the cold. She seemed to have recovered quickly physically—she actually looked healthier than she had in weeks—and if her expression was at times wistful, the thoughts she expressed to me were hopeful. She put an arm around my waist on our hike back to the car, and I hugged her shoulders.

"When we do have a baby, we won't have moments like this," she said. "I guess we'd better enjoy them while we can."

"Sure we will," I said. "We'll just have to get one of those baby backpack things these people all seem to have. It'll be good for us. Like walking with weights attached."

She smiled. "What if we have a baby who hates the outdoors? It's possible, you know."

"Then little Poindexter or Genevieve can sit in the shade while Mommy and Daddy hike," I said, and she laughed.

I took it as a good sign that despite what we'd been through Anna spoke so easily of our future children. She had said she was relieved to know she was capable of pregnancy, and she seemed to be holding on to that thought. I'd spent so much time worrying about her since the miscarriage it was reassuring to know she was okay.

Looking back, I don't know if I can honestly say I was as eager to have children at that time as I had previously been. Vacationing with Anna, hiking and exploring as we'd always loved to do, was serving to highlight exactly how isolated we'd been the past few years. Some part of me was beginning to chafe under the constant worry over the issue. That's not to say I didn't want children; it's just that at some point during the years we'd spent trying to get pregnant, the desire for *having* a baby had somehow gotten lost in the desire to *produce* one.

That wasn't something I could say to Anna, because it wasn't something I was fully aware of, myself. What I did know was I felt more at peace than I had in a very long time. We spent a leisurely evening wandering through the shops of downtown Chattanooga until the sun began to set and the air became too chilly to enjoy.

On the way back to the rustic little cabin we'd rented we stopped for firewood, a nice bottle of Chardonnay, a small block of Gruyère, and some chilled crabmeat. I built a fire while Anna spread a quilt in front of the fireplace and laid out the fixings of our meal. We were quiet as we worked, but it was a comfortable quiet, both of us pleasantly tired after a long day of sun, wind, and hiking.

We drank a toast to our future and reminisced about our past. Later we fell asleep in each other's arms, and although I can't speak for Anna, I was happy, for once, that neither of us had seemed to entertain any thoughts of baby-making.

Chapter 16
April, 2000

Anna did not bear up as well after the loss of our second baby, and neither did I. She turned her grief inward, sitting quietly for long stretches of time, gazing out the window or staring into space. "Give her time," the doctor said. "She's been through a lot these last few months, both physically and emotionally. She needs time to heal."

Cathy came to visit about a month after Anna's second miscarriage, staying for several days, and although I'd never felt at ease around her, Anna seemed to take comfort from her presence, and for that I was appreciative. We hadn't seen much of Cathy over the years; she had a tendency to disappear for long stretches of time. The few occasions she did return to Tennessee she arrived unannounced, showing up on her parents' doorstep with an overnight bag, crashing for a day or two before leaving again, more often than not before Anna and I had even had a chance to see her.

I don't remember how she happened to be in Tennessee so shortly after Anna's second miscarriage, but I can't imagine she made the trip solely for us. I only remember Anna hanging up the phone and turning to me, her expression slightly surprised, to tell me Cathy was coming to be with her. She was touched by that, I could tell, and I was happy for her, relieved at that moment to see something other than the sadness I'd become accustomed to seeing.

To Cathy's credit, she was very kind to Anna during that visit. They sat on the porch swing sipping hot tea and went for walks through the fields and sat up talking late into the night. During the time Anna spent with her sister, I watched her slowly come back to herself. For her part, Cathy seemed to have settled down some by then; aside from a propensity to wander the house at night in nothing more than a t-shirt and panties—a fact I only became aware of when I literally stumbled into her on my way to the kitchen one sleepless night—her behavior was devoid of the overt sexuality that had always marked her interactions with me.

Unlike Anna, I turned my grief outward: I was angry. While Cathy sat with Anna, I went for long runs, my feet pounding the pavement in rhythm to the angry mantra in my head. I was angry at God, or the universe, or whatever higher power had decided to be cruel to Anna. I stayed away from the women for the most part during that week, keenly aware that my emotional turmoil was unhelpful to Anna. I needed to work through my own feelings before I could help Anna with hers, and I was indebted to Cathy for allowing me the space.

By the time Cathy left, at the end of a week, Anna and I were both in a much better place, and I remember thinking it odd that it took Cathy, of all people, to get us there. Anna remarked on it as we sat together in the swing the evening of Cathy's departure.

"That's the closest I've ever felt to my sister," she said. "It was nice to have her here."

"It was," I agreed. "And she didn't even grope my ass."

Anna laughed, and it was music to my ears. I pulled her close, and she rested her head on my shoulder. In the distance crickets chirped and somewhere behind us I heard a lone tree frog calling for a mate. "Maybe it was good for her to see me in a vulnerable state," Anna said. "Is that a terrible thing to say?"

"I'm not sure," I answered her, a little surprised by the statement. "What do you mean?"

"I just mean misery loves company. There's some truth to that, you know. I think Cathy has been miserable most of her life. Maybe it made her feel closer to me, seeing me miserable, too." Leave it to Anna to try to figure out the pieces.

I thought about what she had said. "Maybe," I said, "but that's a pretty sad assessment, don't you think? Your sister is finally nice to you because you're as miserable as she is."

"I don't know, Phillip," she said, nudging the swing into motion with one foot. "I don't think she can help it. No one would want to live the way Cathy lives, always angry, keeping things stirred up. I remember my mother once saying she'd had a cousin like that, sort of a black sheep of the family. I've never met her; I think Mom cut ties with her as soon as she was able. But I've heard stories. According to Mom, this cousin lived to create controversy."

"We probably all have a relative like that," I said. "The one people dread seeing at family dinners because you just know there'll be some sort of scene. In my family it's Aunt Alma, Mom's sister. Remember how she was at our wedding? The flowers were too wilted, the cake was too dry. Some people just like to complain."

"I guess so," she said. "But in my family it seems to be more than that. It goes beyond being grumpy. There are relatives on my mother's side I've never met, did you know that? A distant branch Mom doesn't like to talk about. A *criminal element*," she bracketed the words with air quotes. "Bootleggers from way back, so the story goes, from some unheard of little town in West Virginia. Mean people, very rough. Maybe there's some genetic strain that works its way through the generations."

"Your family is predisposed to be mean?" I asked, teasing her, but she ignored the playful note in my voice.

"Not everyone," she said. "Not my mother, obviously, and I hope not me. But Cathy has a mean streak, you can't deny that. I feel guilty saying that, after she was so good to me this last week, but the whole time she was here I knew not to let my guard down."

"That's understandable, honey. One nice week doesn't make up for years of mistreatment."

"This is going to sound terrible," she said, as if apologizing in advance, "but on the rare occasions when Cathy is nice, I can't help but wonder what she's after."

I shrugged. "Don't you think it's possible she just wants to be nice?"

"No," she said, and shook her head. "I told you it was going to sound terrible. But seriously, Phillip, I've never felt Cathy really cares about other people. She cares about what they can do for her, or what she can get from them, but she doesn't care about them in any real sort of way."

"That's sad," I said, "and a little scary."

"It is," she agreed. "Does it worry you?"

"Cathy? Of course not. She can't hurt us, babe."

"Not Cathy so much as knowing somewhere in my family history I have ancestors who were bad people. Mean people. What if there is a genetic component?"

I pulled back to look at her. "What exactly are you asking me, Anna? If I'm worried you'll turn into a moonshine swigging maniac? Or that we'll give birth to *The Bad Seed*?"

"Something like that," she said. "Either one, or both."

"No," I said, turning sideways to face her in the swing. "To both questions. I'm not worried. Not in the least. If anything, it's kind of sexy to think of you running 'shine through secret mountain passes in the dark of night. Promise me if you ever go into the business, you'll start wearing overalls. I'd like that."

She studied my face before leaning against me with a sigh. "Okay," she said. "But promise me if you ever see anything that worries you, you'll let me know. Anything at all."

"I promise," I said, "but I'm fairly certain that's not going to happen."

I had the distinct impression Anna was trying to tell me something in her quiet way. In spite of the emotional turmoil of that time, Anna had always been a centered person. Brian's depiction of her sitting quietly on a mountain and thinking wasn't too far off the mark. She wasn't given to outward displays of intense emotion, particularly negative emotion. I couldn't imagine any circumstance under which Anna might share a part of Cathy's temperament, but I knew Anna well enough to know her mentioning it to me indicated she was concerned.

"What's made you wonder about all this?" I asked, slapping at a mosquito and doing my best to sound only casually interested.

"Oh, just … everything." I felt her breath against my neck. "This has been hard, Phillip."

I heard the catch in her voice and reached my other arm around her, hugging her close. "I know it has, baby. I'm sorry."

She wiped away a tear. "I think it's *too* hard, Phillip. My body, the hormones, I'm up, I'm down, it's like a yo-yo. I'm on top of the world, thinking we're finally going to have a baby, and then the crash … I don't think I can do it anymore. I don't think I want to."

We were thirty-three that summer, I just a few months older than she, and we'd been hoping for a baby for years by that point. Beyond hoping, really; as I had begun to realize on our trip to Chattanooga, our desire to have children had dominated our marriage, leaving little room for anything else. We'd spent countless hours at medical appointments, undergoing tests, counting days, finally experiencing euphoria, and then, as Anna said, crashing.

I found myself agreeing with Anna, grateful to her for saying aloud what I'd been afraid to admit. I was ready to refocus on our lives, and I was unwilling to put her through any more failed pregnancies. At that moment, as Anna cried quietly against my shoulder, the last thing I wanted was for her to be pregnant.

Jeffrey was born ten months later.

Chapter 17
Ripley, Tennessee
December 21, 2012: Trial Transcript

Court Clerk: Can you state your name for the record, please?

Cathy Tyler: Cathy Suzette Tyler.

The Court: Your witness, Mr. Young.

Prosecutor: Thank you, Your Honor. Ms. Tyler, you are Anna Lewinsky's younger sister, is that correct?

Cathy Tyler: Yes.

Prosecutor: Are there any other siblings?

Cathy Tyler: No.

Prosecutor: Where do you reside, Ms. Tyler?

Cathy Tyler: In Munford. Just outside of Memphis.

Prosecutor: And what was your father's name?

Cathy Tyler: Michael Tyler.

Prosecutor: And he is deceased, is that correct?

Cathy Tyler: Yes. He died right after Anna did, of a heart attack. The stress of her death …

Defense Attorney: Objection. Witness is speculating. Move to strike that last part.

The Court: Sustained. Ms. Tyler, just answer the questions, please.

Prosecutor: And what is your mother's name, Ms. Tyler?

Cathy Tyler: Connie Tyler.

Prosecutor: And she lives with you, correct?

Cathy Tyler: Yes. It's her house. It's where Anna and I grew up.

Prosecutor: Ms. Tyler, do you know the defendant seated there at Counsel's table?

Cathy Tyler: Yes.

Prosecutor: Tell the Court how you know the defendant.

Cathy Tyler: He is … was … my brother-in-law.

Prosecutor: And how long have you known him?

Cathy Tyler: I think twenty-two, no, twenty-three years now.

Prosecutor: What year did you meet him?

Cathy Tyler: Nineteen-eighty-nine, when he started dating my sister.

Prosecutor: He married your sister, didn't he?

Cathy Tyler: Yes.

Prosecutor: What was the date of the wedding?

Cathy Tyler: September 23, 1989.

Prosecutor: Were you in the wedding?

Cathy Tyler: Yes. I was the maid of honor.

Prosecutor: Where did the wedding take place, Ms. Tyler?

Cathy Tyler: At my parents' house. The one in Munford.

Prosecutor: How long was your sister married to the defendant?

Cathy Tyler: It would have been twenty-three years last September.

Prosecutor: And how would you characterize their marriage?

Defense Attorney: Objection. Vague. The witness can't possibly characterize ...

The Court: Sustained. Rephrase your question, Counselor.

Prosecutor: Did you ever witness your brother-in-law, Mr. Lewinsky, being unfaithful to your sister?

Cathy Tyler: I witnessed him attempting to be unfaithful. Whether or not he ever succeeded, I couldn't say.

Prosecutor: In fact, Mr. Lewinsky made a pass at you, didn't he?

Defense Attorney: Objection. Leading the witness.

The Court: Sustained. Rephrase.

Prosecutor: Can you tell the Court what happened September 14, 1989?

Cathy Tyler: That was the week before Anna and Phillip—Mr. Lewinsky—were married. I was home that week, in Munford, helping Anna and my mother make plans for the wedding. I needed a break, so I decided to go outside for some fresh air. On my way to the door, Mr. Lewinsky, he grabbed me.

Prosecutor: How did he grab you, Ms. Tyler?

Cathy Tyler: He … he grabbed me by the hips and squeezed. He put one hand on each of my hips and pulled me against … pressed my front against his groin.

Prosecutor: You're saying the defendant, Mr. Lewinsky, made a pass at you in your parents' home just one week before marrying your sister?

Defense Attorney: Objection. Leading, asked and answered.

The Court: Sustained.

Prosecutor: That wasn't the only time Mr. Lewinsky made sexual overtures towards you, was it?

Defense Attorney: Objection. Leading the witness.

The Court: Overruled. I'll allow it. You can answer, Ms. Tyler.

Cathy Tyler: No.

Prosecutor: What happened the week of April 10, 2000?

Cathy Tyler: Anna, my sister, had just had a miscarriage. I went to stay with her, to … to help her. One night after she went to bed, Phillip—Mr. Lewinsky—grabbed me in the dark. I had gotten up to get a drink of water. I wasn't … I wasn't fully dressed. I wasn't expecting to see anyone, but maybe I should have known, after what he'd done before …

Defense Attorney: Objection. Narrative. Motion to strike that last part.

The Court: Overruled. Continue.

Cathy Tyler: I only had on a t-shirt and underwear, and I was going down the hall, going back to bed after getting a drink of water in the kitchen, when all of a sudden he was there. He shoved into me, knocked me against the wall. Then I felt his hands on me … on my … on my breasts. He was feeling my breasts. He was so rough … he hurt me …

Prosecutor: Are you okay, Ms. Tyler?

Cathy Tyler: I'm … I'm fine. It's just hard to talk about.

Prosecutor: Your Honor, if it pleases the Court, can we adjourn and continue this after lunch?

The Court: We'll take a short recess and come back at one o'clock. Counselor, you need to get your defendant under control over there.

Chapter 18
Ripley, Tennessee
June 3, 2012: The arrest

"I hadn't known about the miscarriages," Brian repeated, "but now that I do, a lot of things make sense. Anna didn't look well when I came to see you. Difficult pregnancy, you said, but even at the time I thought it was more than that. She must have been exhausted, Phil. Three pregnancies in such a short time, not to mention the heartbreak. I wish I'd known. I wish you had told me."

She was exhausted, yes, and quietly sad. I had not known how to comfort her. It was a very trying time, and though we hadn't known it, the worst was still to come.

"We didn't see the point in telling anyone about the miscarriages," I said. "Our families knew, of course, but no one else did. Anna was private, you know that. She had been through so much; we both just wanted to put it behind us the best we could and move forward."

"And then Jeffrey," he said.

"Yes. And then Jeffrey."

"Not now, Phillip," he said, and I looked at him, noting for the first time how worn he seemed. He sat across from me, elbows on the table, hands cradling his face. An image flashed through my mind, a picture of a much younger Brian standing with elbows propped on the fence enclosing the practice field. He had done that often our sophomore year, watched his old teammates practice without him.

In the beginning they'd come over to speak with him, invite him to join them after practice, but after a while they moved on, leaving Brian to watch them alone. It must have been hard, I reflected, being left behind. But Brian never spoke of it, and by our junior year he no longer haunted the practice field.

Something in his expression as he regarded me across the scuffed table reminded me of that time. Maybe it was because in both instances he'd lost what he'd come to regard as family.

Brian hadn't wanted to speak of his loss back then, and he didn't want me to speak of it now. He didn't want me to speak of Jeffrey.

"I'll come tomorrow," he said, standing. "I just need some time to think about all this, Phil. It hasn't sunk in; it's too much."

I nodded. "Will you see Peter?"

"Of course. And I'll do some checking, look into a lawyer for you."

I stood as he hoisted his briefcase and motioned for the guard. "We'll get through this, Phil," he said. "We'll figure it out."

That was Brian, aligning himself with me as he always had. I watched him go before the guard snapped the cuffs back on and led me away. Truthfully, at that moment I didn't see how Brian could help me. He looked as lost as I felt.

Chapter 19
September, 2000

When the by-now-familiar symptoms presented again, just a few short weeks after Anna's second miscarriage, we agreed to tell no one. We didn't want to get our families' hopes up again only to have them dashed, but it was more than that. We also didn't want to have to make that terrible phone call again, the one signifying the end of everything. The second time had been painful enough; I couldn't imagine a third.

There was no joy in the pregnancy those first months. I know how that must sound, but by that point we had already accepted Anna would not carry to term. Whereas in the past we'd made plans to decorate the nursery, this time we made plans for the inevitable trip to the hospital. Anna kept a small overnight bag packed and in the car, not in anticipation of a midnight trip to the hospital to meet our new baby, but because the previous two times I'd had to return home for a change of clothes lest Anna take leave of the hospital wearing the same bloody clothes in which she'd arrived.

As with the previous two pregnancies, Anna was horribly sick the first couple of months. Because of her history, the doctor had her scheduled for a check-up every two weeks, but while she dutifully went, she refused to discuss the severity of her nausea with the doctor. "What's the point, Phillip? They'll tell me to drink plenty of fluids and rest. We both know what's going to happen. By the third month I'll feel better. And then it'll all be over."

At ten weeks, as she approached the time her previous pregnancies had ended, they conducted an ultrasound. While I could just make out the steady flutter of our baby's heart, Anna refused to look. "I don't want to get attached to a baby I'll never meet," she said, and she turned her face to the wall.

This was a new Anna, one I'd not previously met. I was alarmed by the bitterness in her voice, but at the same time, I understood. After all, I'd had the same thoughts. What bothered me most was Anna's quiet anger towards me, yet I understood that, too. I was the one who had impregnated her; therefore, I was the one responsible for the upcoming heartbreak.

She was distant from me, and if I'm honest, I have to admit I was somewhat relieved by her cool-ness. I had no idea how to comfort her. It was an aw-ful situation; I felt guilty about her pregnancy, worried for her health, terrified of the aftermath, and unable to fix any of it. We were quiet those first months, cir-cling each other in a holding pattern of sorts, both fully expecting a tragic ending somewhere ahead, but unable to predict exactly when it would occur.

This is the shape Brian found us in when he finally chose to visit. We weren't expecting him; it had been several months since he and I had spoken, not since my trip with Anna to Lookout Mountain. Anna was asleep when he arrived; she slept a lot in those days. She was not teaching any classes that quarter; she had arranged for some time off even before finding she was pregnant again. Most mornings she was still in bed when I left, and most evenings I found her on the couch with a blanket when I returned. I did not begrudge her the rest, nor did I begrudge her the mental escape sleeping provided.

I was outside walking the perimeter of our property early in the morning before leaving for work. We had some fences that needed mending; kids from down the road had taken advantage of the openings to four-wheel on our land, and I planned to stop and buy the needed materials on my way home at the end of the day. I'd just stood from measuring a crossbeam when I saw the flash of sun on glass and squinted to see Brian's sleek sedan turning off the main road. He wound his way up the long driveway, and I walked across the field to join him. I was always happy to see Brian, but that morning, watching him unfold himself from the car and turn in my direction, I nearly had to restrain myself from galloping across the lawn. So glad was I to see him it didn't immediately register that Sylvie wasn't with him. Sylvie had played such a small part in our lives I'd nearly forgotten that she *should* be.

"Brian!" I held out my hand for our customary shake and he grasped it, pulling me in for a quick slap on the back. "Where's Sylvie?"

"Eh," he said, with a shrug. "She left. Abdicated the marriage, as it were. Decamped, renounced, apostatized. I know, that's a good one, isn't it? Apostatized." He held up a hand as I started to speak. "It's all good, Phillip. It was a mistake from the beginning."

"Come on inside and fill me in." I looked at my watch. "Do you not have to work today?" It was a Wednesday morning, one I would remember forever, as it turned out.

"I took a few days off," he said. "Going to head up to Kentucky Lake for a few days, camp, do some fishing. Some of the stuff I've missed. I just wanted to stop by on the way, let you guys know what's going on. I wasn't sure I'd catch you, but I thought if I made it early enough you might not have left for work yet."

"Hold that thought while I get us some coffee," I said, leading him to the porch. He stopped at the swing, and I hurried inside, glancing in the bedroom to see Anna still asleep. I grabbed a couple of mugs out of the cabinet and filled them from the pot, black for Brian, I remembered, and sugar for me. I placed a quick call to the lab and begged off for the day, citing illness as the reason, and then returned to the porch. In typical Brian fashion, he was in the swing, kicking it nearly high enough to touch the porch ceiling with the toes of his hiking shoes on the upswing.

"If you don't mind me saying, you don't look exactly heartbroken." I held a mug towards him and he dragged his feet across the porch, bringing the swing to a stop.

"It's a relief, Phil." He took a sip from the cup, and then glanced around the yard. "Where's Anna?"

"Still sleeping." I lowered myself to the steps and leaned against a porch column.

"Asleep? This late in the morning? What's wrong with her?"

"Nothing, she's just tired," I said, and then changed the subject. "So tell me what happened."

"It's not so much that anything happened," he said. "More that it didn't. We just didn't fit, you know? We tried; we really did. She's a great lady. She deserves someone who can love her the way she needs to be loved."

"That's very generous of you," I said, blowing the coffee to cool it. It was wonderful to be sitting outside with my buddy, drinking coffee on a beautiful fall morning. For a moment, I could almost put the last year behind me.

"I'm a generous kind of guy," he said, smiling. "It really is okay, Phil. Kind of like correcting a mistake I shouldn't have made in the first place. Now I just feel the need to catch up on all the stuff I missed the last few years. Like you guys." He slurped at his coffee, looked over at me. "Don't you have to go to work?"

"I just called in. It was time for a day off, anyway."

"You didn't have to do that, Phil. I didn't mean to disrupt your day."

"Well, from a purely selfish standpoint, it's really good to have both of you here," said Anna, and we looked over to see her standing by the screened-in storm door. Her hair was disheveled and her old MSU t-shirt hung loosely on her thin frame, but as soon as I saw her, I knew something had changed. It wasn't just that she was smiling; it was more than that. It was that the smile looked real.

Brian stood as she walked onto the porch, enveloping her in a bear hug. She held onto him a second longer than usual, and he looked over at me with a slight frown. I responded with a quick shake of the head. *Don't ruin the moment*, I wanted to say. *You have no idea how rare that smile is these days.*

He turned his attention back to Anna. "Why so skinny?" he asked, pulling back to look at her. "Are you okay?" He turned to me before she could answer. "Is she okay? This isn't our quirky little philosopher." Then back to Anna. "What's going on, Socrates? Why are you so pale?"

I tensed, ready to jump in with a lie, but Anna was looking at me, and she was still smiling. I found myself smiling back, and as I did, a massive weight fell from my shoulders. She was going to tell him. We weren't going to be alone in this anymore. *I* wasn't going to be alone in this anymore.

"I'm pregnant," she said with a shrug and a grin. "Fourteen weeks."

"Oh, my God!" Brian grabbed her in another hug and swung her around before rethinking his reaction. "Oh, no. I'm sorry. Sorry, sorry, sorry." He set her gently back on her feet and smoothed her hair. "Are you okay? Did I hurt you?"

"I'm fine, Brian," Anna laughed, and I relaxed, thinking through the words she'd spoken. Fourteen weeks, she'd said, longer than we'd previously made it, two weeks past the dangerous first trimester. I'd been so caught up in worry I'd lost track of time. I looked at her, a silent question in the air between us.

She crossed the porch and bent to kiss me on the mouth. "Do you know what today is?" she asked, whispering in my ear. I shook my head, pulling away to look at her. "It's the day we have our second ultrasound. I didn't put it on the calendar. I didn't want to think about it, in case … well, you know. But I think we've made it this time, Phillip. I really think we have."

"What are you two whispering about over there?" Brian called from his seat on the swing. "And what kind of service is this, anyway? I need more coffee, and you two have clearly had enough time alone," he said, with a knowing glance at Anna's stomach. "Don't you have any food around here? Did I mention my wife left me? Seems like the least you could do is feed me. Obloquious treatment, I tell you. I expected better."

Obloquious. I had no idea what the word meant, but, dear God, it was good to see Brian.

Chapter 20
November 23, 2000

Thanksgiving that year dawned gray and misty, the kind of Tennessee weather that chills to the bone. That chills most people, I should say. Anna was hot.

"He's like a little furnace," she said, cracking her window open to the damp morning and fiddling with the air vents. We were on our way to the Tyler home in Munford, and Anna seemed intent on freezing me before we made it.

"In that case, can I borrow him?" I asked. "If you're going to keep trying to turn me into a snowman, I need a furnace of my own."

Anna glanced over at me and smiled. "Sorry, babe. He took long enough to get here. I'm keeping him with me as long as I can."

"Then I hope your parents won't mind if I soak in a hot bath when we get there. It might be the only way to thaw out my feet." The only thing I hated more than cold, wet weather was cold, wet feet. "What?" She was staring at me with a bemused expression.

"You're cute when you whine," she said. "It brings out your inner Keats."

"My inner what?"

"Keats. You know, *Ode on Melancholy*. 'Drown the wakeful anguish of the soul,' and all that."

"More than my soul will be drowning if you don't roll up that window," I grumbled. "It's raining."

"Misting," she corrected, but she rolled the window partway up with a sigh. "What do you think about Keats?" she asked.

"Can't say as I think anything at all about him," I said, setting the thermostat on warm and pointing all the vents at me. "I barely remember studying him. Wasn't he the one who wrote all the odes?"

She nodded. "He wrote a few. I seem to remember something about a Grecian urn. But I guess what I'm asking is, what do you think about his take on melancholy?"

I searched my memory. "Was he the one who thought it was a natural part of life?"

"Sort of," she said. "He thought joy and sadness went hand in hand. You couldn't experience joy if you hadn't experienced sadness."

"Makes sense," I said. "But why do you ask? I'm the melancholy one in this relationship."

"You do have your darker moments, don't you? But I don't know if I'd say you're the only one."

I squeezed her hand, the one I was holding across the seat. "It's been a tough time, hasn't it?" She nodded, and I continued. "But maybe that's all past us now. Maybe the future is smooth sailing."

She squeezed me back. "If Keats was right," she said, "we're due some joyful days."

Although Anna had struggled through the early weeks of the pregnancy, she'd seemed to rally with the first trimester safely behind us. We were still cautious, even superstitious, as if we were afraid of jinxing the pregnancy by fully acknowledging it. We hadn't painted the nursery or bought a baby bed, nor had we discussed names.

But we had finally told our families, and they were waiting on the Tyler porch as we turned into the driveway. I raised Anna's hand to my mouth for a quick kiss. "Showtime," I said, and Anna took a deep breath.

"Maybe we shouldn't have told them yet," she said. "I don't want to disappoint them again."

"You are never disappointing," I said, and reached over to hold her chin, forcing her to look at me. "We've had some bad luck, but that's over now. These people are here to celebrate, so bring your belly along and let's introduce them to the guest of honor. Okay?"

"Okay," she said, "just as long as he doesn't try to make an actual appearance."

Several things were memorable about that Thanksgiving. It was the first Thanksgiving Anna's family and mine had spent together under the same roof, a circumstance that was driven by news of Anna's pregnancy. We'd told them just the week before and Anna's mother had proposed a joint holiday-slash-baby-celebration. She volunteered the Tyler home because it was the bigger of the two, and my mother assisted by bringing several dishes and arriving early to help with preparations.

Our families had always gotten along well. In some strange way Mr. Tyler's incessant worrying seemed calmer in the presence of my own boisterous father, possibly because Dad's noisy opining left no opportunity for introspection. Our mothers were more similar than different, and I often thought if they weren't both so introverted, they might have developed a friendship over the years. Although neither was outgoing enough to advance their relationship, they did seem to enjoy the few occasions our families were lumped together.

It was also one of the few holidays we spent without Brian. He'd been invited, of course; he'd remained close to both our families through the years, and I suspected Mr. Tyler still credited him with keeping Anna safe during the months we shared that old apartment in Memphis. He'd planned on coming, right up until the last minute when he got a call from a hospital in a town outside of Nashville. His mother had been admitted in an advanced stage of kidney failure; she was not expected to make it.

Brian had initially been ambivalent about going. "I know she raised me," he'd said when he called to give me the news, "but is that enough? I mean, there's a difference between being raised, and being raised right."

"Don't you think you'll regret it if you don't go?" I asked. "It's your last chance, Brian. You don't want that weighing on your conscience."

"You may be right," he said, "but I'm angry. I've always been angry with her. She basically left me to raise myself while she was out partying, and look where that's gotten her. Now she wants to be with me. That's all I wanted as a kid, you know. To have her want to stay home with me instead of going out to bars with people she called friends. And you know what, Phillip?"

I waited without answering, letting him work through the anger.

"Ten to one she'd still be out partying if she were strong enough to get out of the damn bed."

From what little he'd told me, I suspected he was right. "You're not going for her, Brian," I told him. "You're going for you, so you'll know in the end you did the right thing, regardless of her history of always doing the wrong one."

"Damn, Phil," he said. "If you put it that way, I guess I have to go." So he did, booking a short flight out of Memphis and promising to call us with an update when he got a chance.

The only pall over the holiday was, not surprisingly, created by Cathy. She, too, was missing in action, but she hadn't bothered with a phone call to explain her absence. To make matters worse, her cell phone was apparently off, and she hadn't responded to any of her mother's messages. Whereas Mrs. Tyler's imagination naturally jumped to the worst of conclusions, Anna was more pragmatic.

"This isn't the first time she's done this, Mom. She's probably sleeping, or she just forgot to charge her phone. I'm sure she'll show up soon." If she resented her younger sister upstaging her on what was supposed to be a celebration of our baby, she didn't show it, no doubt used to it by then. "You finish mashing the potatoes," she told her mother, drying her hands on a dishtowel, "and I'll try to reach Cathy."

Cathy answered on the first ring, as if expecting the call, and Anna stepped onto the back porch to continue the conversation. Not five minutes later she was back, going to stand beside her mother at the counter and placing an arm around her shoulders. "She said she's not feeling well," Anna told her. "She thinks she may be feverish, and she doesn't want to take a chance around me and the baby. She said to eat without her and she'll stop by this evening for leftovers after we're gone."

"Well, now, that was thoughtful of her," said Mrs. Tyler. "Poor thing. There's a bug going around; one of the ladies at church missed Bible study because of it. I'll save her a plate for later."

Anna patted her mother's back before coming to lean against the counter beside me. "She also said I'd have plenty of people fawning over me without her contribution," she whispered, out of range of her mother's hearing.

"Seriously?"

"That's what she said."

"Good Lord," I replied. "That's ridiculous. Do you think that's the real reason she isn't coming?"

"Could be," said Anna. "She doesn't like not being the center of attention."

"I'm sorry, Anna." I pulled her close for a hug. "Don't let it bother you; it isn't worth it."

"It doesn't bother me, really," she said. "It's actually kind of a relief. At least we know no one will throw the turkey against the wall this year."

I hadn't heard that story before, but dinner was announced before I could ask for details. Surrounded by the hubbub of family and the temptation of food, my curiosity was soon forgotten. I took my seat between Anna and Mrs. Tyler and gazed around the table. Next year, I found myself thinking, the seating arrangements would be different. Our baby would be nine months old by then. I looked at Anna, beside me, engrossed in conversation with my mother. Next year, we'd have a high chair between us. Our son would be the center of attention. I'd gently scold him not to smear the mashed potatoes in his hair while our parents laughed, and Anna took pictures.

"What are you smiling about?" Mrs. Tyler's question brought me back to the present.

"I was imagining having a nine month old baby at the table," I said, somewhat sheepishly.

She laughed. "I've been doing that all day," she said, "thinking, 'Next year, he can lick the beaters,' or, 'I wonder if he'll like pumpkin pie?' I was even thinking we'll have to buy a playpen so he can have a safe place to nap. We'll put it in the spare bedroom off the kitchen so he won't be too far away from us."

"And a high chair," I said. "We'll have to get one. We haven't really bought anything yet, because we wanted to be sure ..." I didn't finish the thought.

"None of that, now," said Mrs. Tyler. "All that's behind us."

"I hope you're right," I said, glancing at Anna. "I don't think she could take it happening again."

Mrs. Tyler followed my gaze. "How's she doing?" she asked, lowering her voice.

"I think she's okay," I said. "Cautious, but okay. We still haven't gotten the nursery ready, but she did mention the other day that she was thinking about a jungle theme. She finally told her coworkers about the baby just yesterday. They want to plan a shower for her, of course, and she hasn't said 'no.' I think she's starting to let herself believe it's actually going to work out."

"Well, good," she said. "But keep an eye on her, Phil." She leaned closer. "I had some trouble myself, you know."

This was news to me. "What do you mean?"

She leaned so close she was nearly whispering in my ear. "I had a miscarriage, too, before Anna. I was scared to death when I got pregnant with Anna, afraid it was going to happen again."

"Does Anna know this? She's never mentioned it."

"I thought she did, but now that you ask, I can't say I remember ever talking about it with her. It wasn't something Mike and I brought up to people after it happened. We didn't really discuss those things back then, you know."

"It might help her to know," I said, "if you don't mind talking to her about it. At least she could see that things can still work out in the end."

"I'll talk to her before y'all leave today," she said. "Now I feel bad I didn't talk to her about it sooner. Somehow I just thought she knew, but I don't reckon she does, does she?"

"I'm sure she doesn't," I said. "But was everything okay after that? Was Anna's birth normal? Was she healthy?"

She nodded. "As easy as a birth can be, at least. Anna was a beautiful baby. She was never any trouble at all. I had a little touch of what they called the 'baby blues,' but that didn't have anything to do with Anna, and I got through it soon enough. I was lucky to have my momma come and help me, and I'll be there to help y'all, too. You and Anna will get sick and tired of

having us there, won't they Maria?" She leaned forward to get my mother's attention.

"What's that?"

"I said we'll be there helping take care of this baby so much they'll have to send us home, won't
they?"

"Oh, absolutely! I'm so excited I've already started buying clothes. Sears had a sale on the cutest little
pajamas, and I just couldn't help myself."

Anna smiled at me as our mothers composed a
list of must-haves for the baby. "We really have to get
the nursery put together this weekend," she said.
"We've waited long enough. And his name is Jeffrey.
Jeffrey Daniel Lewinsky."

"Well, of course it is," I said, and Anna leaned
over to kiss my cheek.

Chapter 21
Memphis, Tennessee
February 23, 2001

No matter how prepared a person might believe himself to be, no matter how organized, planned, and scheduled, the moment a woman announces she's in labor, panic ensues. At least, that's been my experience, and judging by the chaos that greeted us in the form of friends and family upon our arrival at the hospital, it seems to be the experience of others, as well.

The hospital paged Dr. Charles Gillespie, who was expecting us, and although it took him a mere fifteen minutes to arrive, I must have aged twenty years before I caught sight of him striding through the door. While he stopped to greet both my parents and Anna's, I bit my lip and did my best not to bodily drag him to Anna's side. Ordinarily, his laidback style put me at ease, but I wasn't used to seeing Anna in pain, and every moment he dallied to speak with our parents felt like an eternity.

Greetings and small pleasantries finally done, he made his way to the end of the bed. "How's Mom doing?" he asked, causing Anna to smile between contractions.

"I think I'm okay," she said. "Ready to meet him, that's for sure. I—" She stopped, overcome by a contraction.

"How far apart are the contractions?"

I answered, because Anna clearly couldn't. "We left the house right after we talked with you, and by the time we got here they were about five minutes apart. But that was over an hour ago. It took forever for us to check in. I was starting to worry we'd be having our baby in the lobby." I stroked Anna's hair as she caught her breath.

"There isn't any *apart*," she said. "They don't stop." She gritted her teeth as another one hit.

"How dilated?" He turned to the nurse.

"About eight centimeters, fully effaced."

Dr. Gillespie was visibly surprised. "Anna, you're about to meet your baby, sooner rather than later. I'll be back as soon as I'm scrubbed in." He turned to go, his exit markedly faster than had been his entry.

"Well," my dad said, "that's our cue to leave. Good luck, honey." He patted her on the leg while my mother kissed her cheek, and then mine. "We'll be praying for you in the waiting room."

"Hold up, Dan," said Mr. Tyler. "We're going with you. Just let me kiss my girl goodbye." He waited for Mrs. Tyler to kiss Anna, then planted his own kiss on her head. "You tell 'em to come get me if you need me, you hear?" he said to me, and I nodded.

"Take good care of her, Phillip," Mrs. Tyler said, hugging me around my waist. "And take care of you, too. Husbands weren't allowed in when I had my babies. I'm glad you're going to be with her." She turned to Cathy. "Ready to go, honey?"

"Most definitely," said Cathy. "This is not really something I want to witness." She waved at Anna. "I'll see you when you're all done."

It seemed as if things happened very quickly after that, though I later realized hours had passed. In the beginning, things appeared to progress smoothly. Anna was certainly experiencing pain, but as the nurse explained, she was too far into the process for an epidural by then. We focused on her breathing as we'd been taught to do in our birthing class, and that seemed to help. I stroked her hair, rubbed her back, and offered her ice chips.

I vaguely remember the nurse suggesting Anna walk around the room to speed along the process, and Anna did her best to comply. It was I who, walking with Anna and watching helplessly as one contraction after another wracked her body, led Anna back to the bed and told the nurse we would no longer be walking. It was difficult to witness Anna's discomfort, but we had been prepared for what she would go through, to the extent any new parents can be; we knew the stages of delivery, and while it was terrifying in its way, the labor itself didn't raise any red flags of alarm for either of us.

I felt the first prickling of apprehension shortly after Anna began pushing. I remember Dr. Gillespie frowning, calling the nurse over to consult, but all he said to us was, "He's an active little guy, isn't he? Looks like he changed position just as he started to enter the birth canal. I see little fingers, wedged there beside his head. He's waving at us."

Anna was trying to sit, and I crawled onto the bed behind her to support her. She was slick with sweat; the sheets were soaked. "What does that mean?" she asked. "Is the baby okay?"

Dr. Gillespie nodded towards the machine monitoring the baby's heartbeat. "So far so good," he said. "But it means you've got a little more pushing to do. If nothing changes, and it isn't likely to at this point, the head and arm will emerge first. I'm going to give you a little injection here, Anna. I doubt you'll even feel it, with all you've got going on. Then we'll do an episiotomy, just a little incision to help accommodate the baby's new position. Don't push," he warned, as Anna's body began to bear down again. "Dad, help with her breathing."

The nurse came around and took Anna's hands. "You don't want to push while the doctor makes the incision," she said. "When you feel the urge to push, I want you to breathe like this," she demonstrated a series of puffs. "Dad, help her with that, okay? Let's try it."

"All good," said Dr. Gillespie as Anna and I wound up another session of puffing. "And his heartbeat looks strong. In a situation like this, there's always the possibility he'll need a little help joining us. If we see a change in heartbeat or if he's stressed we'll use forceps to help him along. I don't want you to be alarmed if that happens. It looks much scarier than it is. I'm also going to have the nurse call for some extra help in case we need it. Jenna?" He turned to the nurse. "See if Dr. Wilmington is still here, would you? If he is, ask him to stick around. And give Dr. Lindsey a call, too."

He turned back to us. "Dr. Wilmington is a neo-natologist. He was here on a consult earlier, and it'd be nice to have him available. Dr. Lindsey is an orthopedic specialist. Given the positioning of the baby's arm, I'd like Dr. Lindsey to look him over once he's here, just to be safe."

Dr. Gillespie's command of the situation reassured us, and as the nurse began making calls, Anna was once again encouraged to push. We were certainly anxious, both of us, but I don't think we knew enough to be truly afraid. We had complete trust in Dr. Gillespie and his colleagues, who began filing into the room shortly after the calls went out. They struck us as cautious but confident, clearly at ease and in control of the situation.

Sometime later—the parameters of time seemed elasticized that night—Dr. Gillespie called our attention to the machine that displayed our baby's heartbeat. "His heartbeat has slowed some," he said. "A little slowing is to be expected once the baby enters the birth canal, but I'm not comfortable with the current rate. I'm going to use forceps to help him along, so just relax, Anna. Phillip, help with her breathing. You'll be meeting your baby soon."

We did as Dr. Gillespie instructed. I breathed along with Anna, my mood balancing somewhere between excitement and fear, until my attention was arrested by his quick intake of breath.

"Jenna," he said sharply, and the nurse rushed to his side. He spoke too quickly for me to understand what he said; the terms were unfamiliar. As soon as he finished speaking, the doctors who had gathered around the perimeter of the room jumped into action.

The room was packed with people, some pushing machines, others pushing carts loaded with supplies.

I was still behind Anna at that time, holding her as she lay propped against my chest. I eased from behind her and scooted forward to try to see what was going on, and it was then that I saw what had previously been outside my line of vision. In the center of the flurry of doctors behind Dr. Gillespie lay Jeffrey—quiet, covered with blood, and utterly still.

Chapter 22
Ripley, Tennessee
December 21, 2012: Trial Transcript

The Court: All right, we're back on the record in the Lewinsky matter. Let the record show the jury is present. Mr. Lewinsky is present with his counsel, and the people are represented by Mr. Bradley Young. I'll ask counsel for both sides, is there anything we need to discuss before Ms. Tyler continues her testimony?

Defense Attorney: No, Your Honor. Thank you.

Prosecutor: No, Your Honor.

The Court: Then Mr. Young, your witness was previously sworn in, and you may proceed.

Prosecutor: Thank you, Your Honor. Good afternoon, Ms. Tyler.

Cathy Tyler: Good afternoon.

Prosecutor: When we adjourned for lunch, you had just finished telling us about a couple of incidents in which the defendant made sexual advances towards you.

Defense Attorney: Objection. Leading, asked and answered.

The Court: Sustained.

Prosecutor: Ms. Tyler, have there been instances in which you witnessed the defendant behaving aggressively towards Anna?

Cathy Tyler: Yes. I was always afraid of him.

Defense Attorney: Objection.

The Court: Sustained. Ms. Tyler, just answer the question as it's asked.

Prosecutor: When was the first time you witnessed Phillip Lewinsky acting aggressively towards Anna?

Cathy Tyler: On the day their first baby was born.

Prosecutor: Your sister had her first baby February 23, 2001, is that correct?

Cathy Tyler: Yes.

Prosecutor: And it was a boy.

Cathy Tyler: Yes.

Prosecutor: Can you tell us the child's name?

Cathy Tyler: Jeffrey Daniel Lewinsky.

Prosecutor: Was it a difficult birth?

Defense Attorney: Objection. Calls for speculation. Was the witness in the delivery room?

The Court: Sustained.

Prosecutor: In what hospital was the baby born, Ms. Tyler?

Cathy Tyler: Baptist Memorial in Memphis.

Prosecutor: Okay, and to your knowledge, were there complications related to the baby's birth?

Cathy Tyler: Yes.

Prosecutor: And on what do you base your answer?

Cathy Tyler: On the report given to me and my family when Jeffrey was born.

Prosecutor: Who gave you that report, Ms. Tyler?

Cathy Tyler: Dr. Charles Gillespie, Anna's OBGYN.

Prosecutor: Was he present at the birth?
Cathy Tyler: Yes, he was.

Prosecutor: Were you present at the birth?

Cathy Tyler: I was in the waiting room with my parents and Mr. and Mrs. Lewinsky.

Prosecutor: Did the attending physician inform you of the baby's birth?

Cathy Tyler: No, it was a nurse. We'd been waiting for hours by that time. She came out and told us the baby had been born, but there had been some complications. She said Phillip wanted us all there for the doctor to tell us what was wrong.

Prosecutor: So you went to your sister's room?

Cathy Tyler: I did.

Prosecutor: And what did you find when you arrived in your sister's room?

Cathy Tyler: My sister was out of it.

Prosecutor: Tell the Court what you mean by "out of it."

Cathy Tyler: She was exhausted, sort of sleeping off and on, but alert some of the time. She was very pale, very weak. She was hooked up to some machines; I don't know what they were.

Prosecutor: Who else was present in her room?

Cathy Tyler: Well, my parents and Phillip's parents went with me to Anna's room. When we got there Phillip was already there with Dr. Gillespie. And someone else, a nurse, I think, was there monitoring Anna.

Prosecutor: Where was the baby?

Cathy Tyler: I don't know exactly where he was. He wasn't in the room.

Prosecutor: So your sister, Anna, was "out of it," as you say, and the baby had been removed from the room. What had happened?

Defense Attorney: Objection. Seriously, Bradley? The witness can't possibly answer that in a credible manner. Not only was she not there, she's not a medical expert. For heaven's sake.

The Court: Sustained, Counsel, but I'm perfectly capable of making my ruling without an extended lecture from you. A simple "objection" will suffice. As for you, Mr. Young, I'm certain you know the correct procedure.

Prosecutor: Sorry, Your Honor. Ms. Tyler, did the attending physician, Dr. Gillespie, give a report once you'd entered the room?

Cathy Tyler: Yes. Phillip asked him to share the information with all of us.

Prosecutor: And what did Dr. Gillespie say?

Cathy Tyler: He said that Jeffrey was in distress when he was born. He had been in sort of the wrong position, with his arm up by his head when he entered the birth canal. At first his heartbeat was fine, all the way up until … well, until right before he was born. Then it dropped, and Dr. Gillespie used forceps to help get him out. He said Jeffrey showed evidence of a stroke when he was born, because he wasn't moving on one side.

Prosecutor: What was the defendant—Mr. Lewinsky—what was his reaction when the doctor finished speaking?

Cathy Tyler: He was sitting on the bed with Anna, up by her head, and he just…he balled up his fist and hit the wall right over her head. It scared me to death.

Defense Attorney: Objection. Your Honor …

The Court: Sustained. Ms. Tyler. Again, just answer the questions.

Cathy Tyler: I'm sorry, Judge.

Prosecutor: What did Anna do when Phillip hit the wall?

Cathy Tyler: She ducked her head and started crying. She was saying, "I'm sorry, Phillip. I'm sorry." She thought he was mad at her, I guess, because she might have made the baby sick.

Defense Attorney: Objection and move to strike that last statement. The witness can't speak to what Mrs. Lewinsky was thinking.

The Court: Sustained. The jury should disregard the witness's last remark. Mr. Young, do you have further questions for this witness?

Prosecutor: Not at this time, Your Honor.

The Court: Any questions from the Defense?

Defense Attorney: Just a few, Your Honor.

The Court: You may proceed.

Defense Attorney: Ms. Tyler, you testified that you've known the defendant for twenty-three years, is that correct?

Cathy Tyler: That's right.

Defense Attorney: When is the last time you spoke with Mr. Lewinsky?

Prosecutor: Objection. Immaterial.

The Court: I'll allow it. Proceed, Counselor.

Defense Attorney: I'll ask you again. When is the last time you spoke with Mr. Lewinsky?

Cathy Tyler: I don't know. It's been awhile.

Defense Attorney: Within the last year?

Cathy Tyler: No.

Defense Attorney: The last five years?

Cathy Tyler: No, but what—

Defense Attorney: Isn't it true that the last time you spoke with Mr. Lewinsky was March 5, 2001? Over ten years ago, just three days after Jeffrey's funeral?

Cathy Tyler: That could be right. I didn't keep up with it.

Defense Attorney: You've had no contact with the defendant for over a decade, is that correct?

Cathy Tyler: I suppose it is.

Defense Attorney: And yet, you feel you know him?

Prosecution: Objection. Argumentative.

The Court: Sustained. You've made your point, Counselor. Move on.

Defense Attorney: Ms. Tyler, isn't it also true that on that day, March 5, 2001, you had an argument with Anna, and at her insistence, Mr. Lewinsky ordered you to leave their home?

Cathy Tyler: Yeah, but that was a misunderstanding. She was upset; she wasn't herself, or she'd never have done that. She—

Defense Attorney: Were you angry with him at that time?

Cathy Tyler: Well sure. Wouldn't you be? I was only trying to help my sister.

Defense Attorney: Isn't it true you've been angry with him ever since?

Cathy Tyler: I don't know if you could say I've been angry. I don't like him, that's for sure. He has no business trying to raise my sister's child.

Defense Attorney: Do you dislike him enough to embark on a campaign against him?

Prosecution: Objection. Inflammatory.

The Court: Sustained.

Defense Attorney: No further questions, Your Honor.

Chapter 23
Ripley, Tennessee
June 4, 2012: Arraignment

True to his word, Brian returned to the jail early the next morning, just after roll call. I hadn't slept, of course, my mind intent on wandering through dark and dangerous territories. Brian didn't look as if he'd fared much better. His appearance frightened me, and my thoughts immediately went to Peter. "How is he?" I asked, before the guard had even removed my cuffs. "How's Peter?"

Brian nodded his thanks to the guard and took a seat across from me, rubbing at the same scar that had held his attention the previous day. "Not well, Phil. There was some ligament damage to his wrist from the break, and his sternum was fractured. There's a lot of bruising, major contusions, but no myocardial rupture, thank God. He made it through surgery, but he hasn't regained consciousness."

"I can't lose another son," I said, but what I meant was, *I can't survive the loss of another son.*

Brian resumed, as if I hadn't spoken. "Phil, even if he survives, the lack of oxygen—"

"But he was breathing," I interrupted him. "He was breathing when they took him from me."

"There's a witness who's come forward."

"I don't care about witnesses right now. I need—"

"She told police she saw you striking Peter."

"What? I never—"

"She says she saw you hitting Peter in the chest."

"No!" I jumped up and behind the glass, the guard moved forward.

"Sit down," Brian hissed, holding up a hand to the guard. "Trust me, showing anger right now will not help you."

"But Brian," I said, sitting, leaning towards him, "I swear to you, I did not hit Peter. He was … he couldn't …" I stopped, willing myself to calm down. "When I got him, he wasn't breathing. His heart … I couldn't detect a heartbeat. I gave him CPR, Brian, and it worked. He was breathing when they took him from me."

In the resultant silence I could hear the ticking of Brian's watch. Outside the room, I heard footsteps, and I imagined people going about their day, making phone calls, running errands, coordinating dinner plans. For an instant the world shifted and I envisioned a chasm, dark and yawning, just out of view under the ground upon which those people walked. They had no idea it was there, waiting for them to slip, but I did, because I'd already fallen into it.

"Cathy wants to petition for custody."

I stared at Brian, unsure I'd heard him correctly. "Of Peter? You can't be serious."

"Unfortunately, I am."

"First off, custody isn't up for grabs. I'm his father, and I plan on it staying that way. Second, she's crazy, Brian. You know she is. She doesn't care about Peter. Hell, she didn't even care about Anna. And you can't have forgotten how she was after Jeffrey died. She upset Anna so much I had to order her to leave."

I never learned precisely what Cathy had said to Anna to upset her so. I only remember Anna's raised voice, pleading with Cathy to stop. I ran up the stairs towards our bedroom to find Anna seated in the middle of our bed, hands over her ears, sobbing. Cathy stood over her, fists on her hips, brows drawn into a frown as she turned to me. "I'm only telling her the truth, Phillip," she said. "She just doesn't want to hear it."

"Make her stop!" said Anna, rocking to and fro on the bed. "Just make her stop."

"Get out," I said to Cathy, pointing towards the door and crawling onto the bed to take Anna in my arms. "I don't know what you've done to her, but get out, and don't come back."

"Fine," she retorted. "I'm going. But Anna, you're only fooling yourself if you think this wasn't a blessing in disguise. You don't want to spend the rest of your life caring for an invalid."

"*Out*," I said again, before turning my attention to Anna.

"First off"—Brian held up a finger, mocking my tone and pulling me back to the present—"the way things stand right now, custody is very much up for grabs. You need to face that fact, Phillip, as awful as it is. Second, who else is there? Cathy will likely be the logical choice for the court. Your parents are gone, and Anna's are too old and in poor health. That leaves Cathy.

"The court would always rather place a child with family than with strangers. Provided, of course, the family member is capable, and although you and I know Cathy's a nutcase, she has no criminal record and no documented history of psychological problems, at least not as an adult. To them, she'll look like a grieving aunt stepping in to raise her murdered sister's child."

A sunny autumn morning, the taste of coffee, and Anna. I was suddenly assaulted by a memory of a younger Anna, curls blowing in the wind, sun reflecting off her glasses. I nearly doubled over from the force of my grief. *Whatever I had, Cathy wanted*, I remembered her saying. *And the thing is, it's not as if she really cared about any of it. Whether it was a blouse, a pair of shoes, or a person, she only wanted what I had so I wouldn't have it.*

For the first time, I wondered if I could face what awaited me. Always before, throughout our marriage, Anna and I had faced things together, no matter how difficult the situation. Our losses had been shared. Now I was alone, and I wasn't sure I had either the strength or the desire to go on. I had already lost Anna, and now Brian was telling me I'd lose Peter, too. There was nothing left. I meant what I'd said: I couldn't bear the loss of another son.

"If you have any chance at all, Phillip, you'll have to be honest with me."

"What do you mean, Brian? I'm always honest with you."

"I mean, if we're going to get you out of here, you've got to tell me everything. You can't protect

Anna." He sat back in the chair, studying me. "I think I know where this is going, Phillip, as much as I don't want to. I was up all night thinking about it. Don't get me wrong; you have your faults. You can be too rigid, too uptight, even a little self-centered. But you're not a murderer. Which reminds me, Anna's"—he paused and cleared his throat—"Anna's remains will be tested for evidence of cyanide poisoning."

"Cyanide? Why?"

"Because cyanide was found in a locked safe in your office."

"Brian, I work in a lab. We've done some recent testing with hydroxocobalamin."

"Which is?"

"An antidote of sorts. A natural form of B-12 used in the treatment of cyanide poisoning. Remember last year, the story about the Texas rancher whose cows all died from cyanide poisoning? It was all over the news. Apparently the hybrid grass the cows were fed was the culprit. Lots of plants contain cyanide, but it's usually locked up by the sugars in the plant. The theory is that the drought Texas has been under stressed the grass and caused the sugars to break down, releasing the cyanide."

"So?"

"So we applied for a grant to study the effectiveness of hydroxocobalamin versus that of epinephrine in treating cyanide poisoning in animals." I blew out a breath, frustrated. "This is crazy. Why are we even talking about this?"

"We're talking about it because given that several witnesses have spoken out to say they saw you kill your wife by pushing her off an observation tower, the presence of cyanide in your office raises some questions. If he'd push her off a tower, the question might be, would he also poison her?"

"Brian." I closed my eyes in an attempt to calm down. "I did not poison my wife. You know how much I loved Anna. My work is all documented, and anything in my office was stored according to procedure."

"Okay. That'll help. The D.A.'s office has been having a field day since the discovery, but it sounds as if we've got that covered."

"You're saying you'll be my attorney."

Brian nodded. "I need to consult on a couple of things, make sure I'm not violating any ethical standards. I've got a few calls in already. I may have to assemble a team, let someone else take the lead. Ordinarily I'd tell a client on trial for murder to stop talking, but in your case, I don't think I can help you if you don't tell me everything."

"I know I have to tell you everything, Brian. That's what I've been trying to do. I'd give my life before I'd betray Anna, but I won't give Peter's."

"That's what I'm counting on," said Brian, standing and signaling for the guard. "Come on, Phil. We have an arraignment to go to."

"You're going with me?"

"That's why I'm here."

I stood, too, and held my wrists out for the cuffs, the words *if we're going to get you out of here* ringing in my ears.

Chapter 24
Memphis, Tennessee
February 23, 2001

Jeffrey had been taken from the room. Neither of us had even been allowed to touch him before he was whisked away. Anna was as near hysterical as I've ever seen her; as Jeffrey was wheeled away by a mob of medical personnel she began to sob inconsolably, blaming herself for whatever had gone wrong. I held her and spoke to her, trying to soothe her pain, both physical and mental. Dr. Gillespie ordered something to be added to her IV drip to calm her, and when our families were brought in, Mrs. Tyler climbed onto the bed on Anna's other side and held her. My mother stood behind me, her hand on my shoulder.

I was having a difficult time understanding all that had happened; I struggled to understand what Dr. Gillespie was saying. "Jeffrey is in good hands," he said. "They'll do all they can for him."

"But what happened?" my father asked from where he stood across the room. "Where is he?"

"There were some complications," answered Dr. Gillespie. "The baby changed position just as he entered the birth canal, nothing too serious, but it made both mom and baby work a little harder than would normally be expected. Still, there were no initial signs of fetal distress. His heart rate remained strong until just after he crowned. At that point, it dropped, and I made the decision to use forceps to hasten the birthing process. He had some difficulty breathing on his own, and he's being given oxygen. More concerning, though, is that he presented with right side hemiplegia."

"What does that mean?" asked Mr. Tyler. "Plain English, please."

"It means he may have had a stroke at some point during the delivery."

I heard my mother gasp from behind me, as Anna buried her face against Mrs. Tyler's neck.

"They will do all they can to stabilize Jeffrey. Dr. Wilmington is the very best; we're lucky to have him here tonight."

"Will he be okay?" my mother asked, tightening her grip on my shoulder.

Dr. Gillespie hesitated just a second too long before answering. "It's too early at this point to know the extent of the complications."

As the doctor grasped for the correct response, Anna reached for me, pulling me down beside her. "Go with the baby," she said. "I'll be fine."

"I can't leave you." I couldn't imagine leaving Anna in the state she was in.

"You have to be there for him, because I can't." she said. "He needs one of us to be there." Before I could respond, Dr. Gillespie interrupted.

"You can't go with him, Phil. Not right now. Let the specialists do their jobs, and then we'll see."

"We can't go see him?" my mother asked, and Dr. Gillespie shook his head.

"Jeffrey is a very sick baby," he said, "in a critical state. We have to get him stabilized. Once we've done that, we'll talk about visitation."

What I remember next is pain, shooting through my hand and up my arm. I remember the strangely satisfying explosion of noise as my fist hit the wall. I wanted to demolish the wall, the room, the hospital, and the man who was delivering this news to me, and to Anna. I drew back my arm to hit the wall again, and suddenly I was surrounded by strong arms. They held me still; I couldn't move. I struggled against the imprisonment, but I couldn't break free of those arms.

"I've got you, son," my father said against my ear. "I've got you."

Chapter 25
Ripley, Tennessee
December 21, 2012: Trial Transcript

Court Clerk: State your full name for the record, please.

Dr. Taylor: Christopher Lucas Taylor.

The Court: You may proceed, Mr. Young.

Prosecutor: Thank you, Your Honor. Dr. Taylor, tell us your credentials, please.

Dr. Taylor: I'm a hematologist. I obtained my medical degree from Vanderbilt University School of Medicine in 1979. I completed my residency at the East Tennessee Comprehensive Hemophilia Center at the University of Tennessee in '82 before returning to Vanderbilt to complete my fellowship studies—subspecialty in coagulation—in 1985. I continued on staff at University of Tennessee's Hemophilia Center until 1998 when I accepted a position at St. Jude Research Hospital in Memphis as a hemostasis and thrombosis specialist. I also consult and maintain a small private practice in Memphis.

Prosecutor: Thank you, Dr. Taylor. It was in that capacity—your private consultation work as a hemostasis and thrombosis specialist—that you first met Anna Lewinsky, is that correct?

Dr. Taylor: Yes. I was called to do an emergency consult on a neonate, Mrs. Lewinsky's son, on February 24, 2001. The infant presented at birth with right hemiplegia caused by a suspected cerebrovascular event somewhere within the distribution of the left middle cerebral artery. As the doctors worked to stabilize him, he began to experience recurrent focal motor seizures.

Prosecutor: Can you explain, for those of us without a medical background, what, exactly, that means?

Dr. Taylor: Certainly. It means that upon birth, the baby exhibited signs of paralysis on his right side, indicating some trauma to the left hemisphere of the brain. Shortly thereafter, he began to experience a series of back-to-back seizures. Both conditions could indicate ischemic cerebral infarction, or stroke, caused by a blockage, such as a blood clot.

Prosecutor: Was the baby examined for evidence of a stroke?

Dr. Taylor: He was.

Prosecutor: What was the outcome of that testing?

Dr. Taylor: As was suspected, Diffusion-Weighted MRI, or Magnetic Resonance Imaging, detected a large lesion in the territory of the left middle cerebral artery. In other words, the baby had suffered a stroke within the left hemisphere.

Prosecutor: I am now showing you what's been marked as State's Exhibit 'D' for Identification. Do you recognize this report?

Dr. Taylor: Yes, I do.

Prosecutor: What is this report?

Dr. Taylor: The findings from the Lewinsky baby's Diffusion-Weighted MRI.

Prosecutor: Does this report truly and accurately reflect the findings from the Magnetic Resonance Imaging?

Dr. Taylor: Yes, it does.

Prosecutor: We would ask the Court to admit State's Exhibit 'D' for Identification as State's #5.

The Court: Any objections?

Defense Attorney: No, Your Honor.

The Court: State's Exhibit 'D' for Identification will be introduced into evidence as State's #5.

Prosecutor: Dr. Taylor, what could cause such a serious condition in a newborn?

Dr. Taylor: Several factors can increase the risk of perinatal stroke. Fetal stress, certain infections, disorders of the placenta, congenital heart disease. The more risk factors present, the higher the risk of stroke. But in many cases, a cause is never determined.

Prosecutor: Was a cause determined in the case of the Lewinsky baby?

Dr. Taylor: Yes, it was.

Prosecutor: What was that cause?

Dr. Taylor: Dr. Gillespie, Anna Lewinsky's OBGYN, suspected a genetic cause. Mrs. Lewinsky had had some difficulty becoming pregnant. She had two known spontaneous abortions, or miscarriages, before carrying the child in question to term. After genetic testing it was determined that Mrs. Lewinsky was heterozygous for factor V Leiden.

Prosecutor: And what exactly does that mean?

Dr. Taylor: Factor V Leiden is a genetic mutation that predisposes people to the risk of blood clots. Mrs. Lewinsky was heterozygous, meaning she had inherited the mutated gene from one parent. Women with factor V Leiden have a higher risk of spontaneous abortion. If the condition is known at the time of pregnancy, anticoagulants can be introduced, maybe something as simple as taking baby aspirin during pregnancy. Unfortunately, in Mrs. Lewinsky's case, she was unaware of the mutation.

Prosecutor: Dr. Taylor, I'm showing you what's been marked as State's Exhibit 'E' for Identification. Do you recognize this report?

Dr. Taylor: I do.

Prosecutor: What is this report?

Dr. Taylor: The findings from the Lewinsky family's genetic testing.

Prosecutor: Is this report a true and accurate representation of the results?

Dr. Taylor: It is.

Prosecutor: I ask the Court to admit State's Exhibit 'E' for Identification as State's #6.

The Court: Any objections, Mr. Stone?

Defense Attorney: No, Your Honor.

The Court: State's Exhibit 'E' for Identification will be introduced into evidence as State's #6.

Prosecutor: Dr. Taylor, how would Mrs. Lewinsky's factor V Leiden have affected the infant?

Dr. Taylor: Factor V Leiden is an inherited disorder; Mrs. Lewinsky's mother was also found to have the mutation. Because it's inherited, the infant had a fifty percent chance of also having the mutation. After postmortem testing, it was determined that the Lewinsky baby did, in fact, present with factor V Leiden.

Prosecutor: And this is what led to the stroke?

Dr. Taylor: The risk of clotting increases as risk factors increase. The baby became stressed while still in the birth canal, necessitating the use of forceps. While it's incredibly rare for a baby to present with such a severe cerebral infarction at birth, it is believed that this combination of factors led to the stroke and subsequent death of the Lewinsky baby.

Prosecutor: You met with Mr. and Mrs. Lewinsky to discuss the genetic indications of factor V Leiden, is that correct?

Dr. Taylor: Yes. I met with them in Mrs. Lewinsky's hospital room, where she was being treated with anticoagulants as a safety precaution.

Prosecutor: When was that meeting?

Dr. Taylor: It was February 27, 2001.

Prosecutor: How did the Lewinskys react to the news?

Dr. Taylor: They were understandably upset. They had just lost a child.

Prosecutor: How did Mrs. Lewinsky react?

Dr. Taylor: She wept throughout the meeting.

Prosecutor: And Mr. Lewinsky? What was his reaction?

Dr. Taylor: He was visibly agitated, pacing, running his hand through his hair. He told me none of our testing mattered; they no longer wanted to have children. He stated he planned to have a vasectomy as soon as possible so they would never have to go through something so horrendous again.

Prosecutor: Was that the last time you saw the Lewinskys?

Dr. Taylor: No. I saw Mrs. Lewinsky again.

Prosecutor: When did you see her again?

Dr. Taylor: I saw Mrs. Lewinsky August 25, 2011. She had an appointment scheduled for ten o'clock that morning.

Prosecutor: She wanted to meet with you over ten years later? What was the nature of that meeting?

Dr. Taylor: She was pregnant. She had just found out, and she wanted to discuss her options.

Prosecutor: Was Mr. Lewinsky at the meeting?

Dr. Taylor: No. She stated she wanted to come alone. He did not yet know about the pregnancy. She stated that she wanted to gather information without him, as she was afraid of his reaction.

Defense Attorney: Objection. Hearsay.

The Court: Sustained.

Prosecutor: Let the record state I'm showing the witness what's been marked as State's Exhibit 'F' for Identification. Dr. Taylor, do you recognize these notes?

Dr. Taylor: I do. They're the clinical notes from my meeting with Mrs. Lewinsky.

Prosecutor: Are they a clear and accurate record of that meeting?

Dr. Taylor: They are.

Prosecutor: I'd ask that State's Exhibit 'F' for Identification be introduced into evidence as State's #7.

The Court: Any objections?

Defense Attorney: No, Your Honor.

The Court: Let the record show that State's Exhibit 'F' for Identification will be introduced into evidence as State's #7.

Prosecutor: Thank you, Your Honor. Dr. Taylor, would you please read your note marked item ten, August 25, 2011?

Dr. Taylor: "Patient states she does not want to tell husband about pregnancy. States she is afraid of what he may want her to do. Wants information regarding factor V Leiden and pregnancy in order to make a decision."

Prosecutor: Did she indicate what she was afraid he might want her to do?

Dr. Taylor: No. I assumed she meant he might want her to abort the fetus.

Defense Attorney: Objection! Speculation. Move to strike that last remark.

The Court: Sustained. The jury is instructed to disregard that last remark.

Prosecutor: Did you see Mrs. Lewinsky again after that?

Dr. Taylor: No. No, that was the last time I saw her.

Chapter 26
February, 2001

Jeffrey lived for three days before dying in Anna's arms. I would like to say he died peacefully, because had he done so, that might have offered us some peace, as well. But he didn't. In spite of the phenobarbital prescribed by his doctors, Jeffrey continued to experience seizures, violently and repeatedly, until the moment of his death.

We had known the time was near. Upon our request, Jeffrey was released from the tubes that bound him and handed gently to Anna. We kissed him and stroked him and tried to cram everything we'd thought we'd have an eternity to experience into a few short moments, as if we could wrap our love, and our broken dreams, into a neat package and hand it to him to take with him when he left.

But I was going to teach you to play baseball, I remember saying to him, as if he could somehow stop the journey his body was taking. *I was going to teach you to ride a bike, and tie a tie, and spot the Big Dipper. We were going to go fishing. I was going to teach you to drive, and yell at you for missing curfew, and you were going to roll your eyes and think I was the worst dad ever until you had kids of your own, and …*

I knew immediately he'd passed on, not only because his tiny body was finally at rest, but because Anna turned her face to mine, and in it I saw every thought we'd refused to share, every fear we'd refused to voice. I saw not only into Anna, but into our future. She had just stepped into Dante's dark forest, and the next step, for both of us, was hell.

How to describe the death of one's child? They sent cards, our friends and family did, along with flowers and poems and prayers, and I wanted to burn every last petal and verse. I didn't want to hear about angel wings or butterfly kisses and meeting in the Great Beyond. I was enraged by the idea that empty platitudes and trite rhymes were somehow supposed to fill the void, the raw, gaping, endless *nothingness* left by the death of our baby.

Lest you think I'm ungrateful for the sympathy extended Anna and me during that time, know this: The condolences extended us were real; those who loved us hurt for us. There's no doubt of that. But even as I knew that, I also knew the cards and flowers and poems about grief and loss were also for *them*, a box checked off a list. Death in the family? *Check.* Card sent? *Check.* Casserole baked? *Check.*

It's what we do, as a society. God knows, Anna and I had done it often enough ourselves. We hear of a tragedy and we send gifts; then we go about our business hoping by the next time we see the object of said tragedy, the poor soul has managed to pick himself up and move on before we have to get a good, close look at the ugly truth of his pain. We don't know what to do with it; it frightens us.

I don't blame people for not knowing how to help us; there *was* no way to help us. *What do you need?* they asked. *What can I get for you?* And we shook our heads. *Nothing,* we said, because what else could we say? *We need Jeffrey; could you fetch him for us, please?*

We held a private memorial service, and Jeffrey was laid to rest in the small cemetery of the church to which Anna and I belonged. I had worried that Anna would break, that she would fling herself into the grave along with the tiny casket, but the breaking of Anna was instead a subtle affair; the cracks were fine but deep, much deeper than I realized at that time. The day of Jeffrey's funeral, as well as for weeks afterward, she was on such heavy medication I had to physically keep her on her feet as she sagged against me and cried.

I wonder about that now. I wonder if it was a mistake, letting Anna hide from the pain, dulled by the tranquilizers so readily prescribed by our doctor. Overwhelmed by my own grief, I was grateful for the numbing effect the pills provided her. I could barely deal with my anguish; I couldn't deal with hers. Like friends and neighbors with their sympathy cards, I handed Anna little blue pills, partly to help her through the darkness, partly to ease the added burden of her grief upon me.

If the fracturing of Anna was subtle, my own fracturing was brutal in comparison. The anger I'd felt upon first learning of Jeffrey's condition continued to fuel me. Within hours of the funeral I'd cleared the nursery of furniture, tossing it into the yard and stomping it to pieces in front of shocked family and friends. When my mother rushed to me, begging me to stop, Brian was the one who gently pulled her back. "Let him be," he said to her, enclosing her in his arms. "Let him get it out."

Later, when he found me painting over the monkeys and giraffes Anna had so painstakingly stenciled on the nursery walls, he picked up a brush and set up station on the opposite side of the room, covering the bright, primary colors with broad strokes of dull white. We painted through the night, wordlessly, and by the time the sun began to rise, we'd nearly erased any evidence of a nursery. I suppose I'd thought by doing so I could set back the clock, erase the horror of the past week and reset our lives, starting sometime after the second miscarriage and before the conception of Jeffrey.

It didn't work, of course. As the darkness outside Jeffrey's window turned to light, I raised my brush for one final stroke, one more coating of white over the vivid red of the parrot painted just inside the doorway, and I found myself unable to complete the task. I collapsed against the wet wall, stroking the outline of the paintings Jeffrey would never see, remembering the hours of work Anna had put into getting it *just right*, and I sobbed. Soundlessly, Brian crossed the room to stand behind me, placing a hand on my shoulder until the worst of the convulsions eased and I could catch my breath.

While I raged and stomped and painted, Anna slept, checked on periodically by both her mother and mine. When I think of that time, which I try not to do, I think of myself as having purged the blackness from my soul. My grief and anger were external, on display, and while it wasn't pretty, the outward expression of my fury allowed me to empty myself of the poison.

Anna, on the other hand, took it inward, sleeping, sitting quietly, medicating. I picture her grief as a parasite, burying deep and changing her very composition with none of us—not even Anna—aware of the damage. And like a parasite, there it sat, waiting, as a parasite does, until it could destroy her, and me in the process.

Chapter 27
Ripley, Tennessee
January 7, 2013: Trial Transcript

Court Clerk: State your full name for the record, please.

John Cooper: Jonathan Wesley Cooper

The Court: Let's get started, Mr. Young.

Prosecutor: Thank you, Your Honor. Where do you live, Mr. Cooper?

John Cooper: Just off the highway. Fifty-one North, I mean. The road off the highway is just an old dirt road, Cooper Lane, named after my family because we've lived on it for generations. I'm at 121 Cooper Lane, if you need the exact address.

Prosecutor: Thank you, Mr. Cooper. Do you recognize the defendant over there?

John Cooper: Yes, sir, I do. He's my neighbor to the south, Phil Lewinsky.

Prosecutor: How long have you known Mr. Lewinsky?

John Cooper: Oh, I'd say going on eighteen years now. Let's see … he moved into the old Jones place back in the summer of '95 and Mary Lou—that's my wife—went over to meet them right away, invited them for supper that first night because she knew they wouldn't have had a chance to get everything unpacked and straightened out.

Prosecutor: Did they come for supper?

John Cooper: Yes, sir, they did.

Prosecutor: What was your impression of the defendant, Mr. Cooper?

John Cooper: He's always been a good neighbor. I just can't imagine him doing what they said he did.

Defense Attorney: Objection. Speculation.

The Court: Sustained. Just answer the questions, Mr. Cooper.

Prosecutor: Mr. Cooper, was there a time you witnessed violent behavior on the part of Mr. Lewinsky?

John Cooper: Yes, sir, there was, but I don't—

Prosecutor: Just answer the questions, please, Mr. Cooper. So there was a time you witnessed Mr. Lewinsky acting violently?

John Cooper: Yes, sir.

Prosecutor: Can you tell the Court when that was?

John Cooper: Yes, sir. I remember it exactly because it was the day of the baby's funeral. The wife and I were over at the Lewinsky house paying our respects. It was a bad time. Their little baby hadn't even made it home from the hospital before he died.

Prosecutor: What was the date on which you witnessed Mr. Lewinsky behaving violently, Mr. Cooper?

John Cooper: It was the second of March, 2001. A Friday. They had laid the baby to rest that morning, and some of us, friends, family, neighbors, you know, had gone back to the house with them after it was all over.

Prosecutor: What happened then, Mr. Cooper?

John Cooper: Well, Anna, Mrs. Lewinsky, was in the bedroom, all tore up over what happened with the baby. Some of us were standing in the kitchen, talking, setting out food like you do, when we heard a big noise from upstairs. Next thing you know, Phil was coming down the stairs holding pieces of a crib— more like a baby bed—in his hands. He went out the front door and threw it in the yard, then starting stomping on it, just smashing it into smithereens.

Prosecutor: What happened next, Mr. Cooper?

John Cooper: Well, he just kept bringing stuff out to the yard, smashing it up and cussing at it.

Prosecutor: What was he saying?

John Cooper: Now, you have to understand, he'd just buried his baby boy, so you can't really—

Prosecutor: Mr. Cooper, you'll get to answer questions from the defense attorney in a moment, but right now I just need you to answer my questions. What was Mr. Lewinsky saying?

John Cooper: Well … he was saying he wished Anna had never gotten pregnant. He was saying he'd make sure nothing like that could ever happen again. But, now, you can't—

Prosecutor: Thank you, Mr. Cooper. No further questions, Your Honor.

Chapter 28
Ripley, Tennessee
January 7, 2013: Attorney Consult

I had not expected another visit from Brian. He had made his phone calls and worked his magic, and I had a team of three attorneys representing me, with Brian taking the third position and consulting, coordinating, and—I believe—directing them as needed. In the months following my last meeting with Brian I'd been summoned numerous times to meet with my new attorneys, but only once had Brian been present, on a drizzly day in October, and that was to tell me Anna's father had died of a heart attack the previous night.

I was sorry about his passing; I had liked Mr. Tyler (I had never been able to bring myself to call him Mike). In some ways, I felt closer to him than I had my own father, who had died, along with my mother, in a car crash on I-40 a couple of years after we lost Jeffrey. I wasn't close to Mr. Tyler in an affectionate way, but rather in a sympathetic way. I understood his neurotic tendencies, his proclivity for finding the sliver of danger in any given situation and worrying over it incessantly. I had those same tendencies myself; besides, hadn't he been right in the end?

When, after a long day in court, I was summoned to the little room with the scarred table that January evening, I was surprised to see Brian alone, facing the door, hands in his pockets. I wish I could say I was happy to see him, but as the guard escorted me into the consultation room and removed the cuffs, what I felt was a slight unease. It wasn't that I no longer cared about Brian; rather, I had worked hard to maintain a distant numbness, and the sight of Brian, alone and outside of the courtroom, threatened that.

I suppose it was a coping mechanism; I didn't put thought into it. I arose at the crack of dawn with the other inmates, ate breakfast, answered roll call, and was escorted back to my cell. Due to the egregious nature of my crimes, I was kept in what passed for solitary confinement. While trustees and various other inmates worked during the day, either inside the jail or out, I lay in my cell and made a game of dissociation. The further I could mentally remove myself from my circumstances, the saner I could remain. I suppose it sounds odd to say I saved my sanity by loosening my hold on it, but it's true. My current reality was more than I could bear, so I fashioned a new one, if only in my mind.

In the world I created for myself, I'd attended college abroad instead of settling for the familiarity of Memphis State University. I'd roomed with a nerdy kid named Pierre instead of a jock named Brian. In my make-believe world I majored in math and taught algebra to reluctant college kids in a make-believe town that boasted cobblestone streets and a curious absence of billboards. I lived in a one-bedroom apartment and spent evenings listening to live jazz bands at the town's cultural center and Sundays mornings working crossword puzzles over coffee at a café overlooking the ocean.

It was a very detailed life, this dream world in my head. After all, I had hours, days, weeks, months in which to create it. It soothed me to imagine my dimly lit theater, deliciously cool, and the blue velvet curtains sweeping back to reveal the shiny brass of the jazz bands of my mind. I was calmed as I conjured up the path along the dunes that led to my ocean café. I not only pictured the wildflowers growing alongside the trail, but named them all: evening primrose and morning glory, silky beach pea, sweet beach strawberry.

I don't know where the images came from, the names, the tastes and sights and smells. I don't know if any of it was real. Do such flowers even exist? It's alternately exhilarating and frightening to explore what the mind is capable of when it's in danger of breaking. I could see every grain of sand; I could feel the cold spray of the ocean and the sun against my back.

Of all of those details I labored to create, one remained constant: There was no Anna in my dream town. There were no babies, no Brian, no friends or family at all. I inhabited my town alone save the ghostly figures that took up seats in my imaginary algebra class, perched on wooden stools at the counter of my café, or sat upon the stage of my shadowy theater. It was this detail that soothed me most of all; one cannot lose what one does not have.

I tell you all this by way of explaining my reaction upon seeing Brian the evening I was summoned to the consultation room. Somewhere, beyond the fantasy life I lived while lying alone in my cell, Brian was still my best friend, but to acknowledge that would mean acknowledging everything else, and I wasn't strong enough to do that. If I allowed myself to open that door even the tiniest crack, I'd drown.

I don't know why Brian had chosen to stay away. I think professionalism played a part in it; he didn't want our history to somehow color the outcome of my trial. But I think he also stayed away because, like me, he didn't know how to deal with the emotions my situation brought forth. Unlike me, Brian didn't have the luxury of checking out of this world and creating a more tolerable one.

Whatever his reasons, I was not happy to see him again. The last time I'd seen Brian outside of court, he'd told me of Mr. Tyler's death. I did not believe his visit this time would be any more pleasant.

Chapter 29
Spring and Summer, 2001

I don't remember the specific moment Anna and I looked up from our heartache to realize life continued on. Perhaps it was on a night in June, as we sat on the porch swinging in the cool evening breeze and Anna commented on the lightning bugs flitting across the neighbor's pasture. Or maybe it was on a sweltering weekend in July, when we ventured forth into town to browse around the square, taking in the booths and activities of the local Tomato Festival. What I do remember is that one night as Anna sat on the couch reading, legs curled beneath her and glasses sliding down her nose, looking so much like she had always looked before our lives had become filled with sadness, I gazed at her and felt, for the first time in months, as if I could breathe.

Slowly, slowly, we pulled ourselves out of the fog. One day we found ourselves going for coffee again, another evening found us renting movies and snacking on cheese and wine. Neither of us spoke of Jeffrey, not for months after our resurfacing, both of us, I suspect, terrified of shattering the brittle calm in which we found ourselves. Our friends and relatives had boxed up any baby equipment I hadn't destroyed and carted it off to Goodwill. Blankets, pajamas, and tiny baseball caps had followed suit. An uninformed visitor to our house would have never guessed we had at one time expected a baby.

Our first step back into the world had been to return to work, though neither of us had felt capable. Our bosses and coworkers had been nothing but supportive, and we'd been told to take all the time we needed. The world, however, was unwilling to wait forever, and no amount of time would have been sufficient. It was Brian whose tough love forced us to take the step, the only of our loved ones willing—or able—to challenge the gray wall of grief surrounding us.

"You need a routine," he said to us on a night about three weeks after Jeffrey's death. He had stayed with us more often than not since Jeffrey died, making the long drive to Memphis each morning before the sun was up. It could not have been easy for him.

He had just made it home that evening, where he found us in nearly the same positions in which we'd been that morning, sitting in the darkened living room. I was brooding in the recliner while Anna chose the rocker closest to the fireplace. If Anna had been perpetually hot before Jeffrey's birth, she was unnaturally cold after his death. Brian knelt to add wood to the fire, settling it with the poker before tossing his suit coat onto the couch, rolling up his sleeves, and turning to look at us.

"This is no good," he said, "sitting and brooding like this. You need something to distract you. Something else to demand your attention. Get mad at me if you need to." He raised his voice to cut me off before I could speak. "In fact, *please* get mad at me; that would be better than watching the two of you sink further into depression. Look, I would never tell you it's time to stop grieving. Hell, *I'm* still grieving. You'll always grieve; of course you will. But you also have to live."

He went to kneel of front of Anna, taking her hands in his. "You need to go back to work. Both of you do. Sitting here, in the dark like this, will only make it worse. Phil." He turned to look at me. "You know I'm right."

I did know, and I think a part of me was relieved to hear him say it. I did need to get back to work. I needed to escape the tomblike silence of our house. I needed, as he had said, a distraction from the pain.

The first weeks were difficult, not only for us, but I imagine for our coworkers, too. There is no proper way to express sympathy. To say nothing seems heartless and unsupportive; to say too much is to stir up the emotion the griever is struggling to control. Hugs elicited tears, pitying looks evoked discomfort, hushed conversations led to embarrassment, and avoidance caused hurt feelings. *It's God's will, time heals all wounds, part of a greater plan, you'll have another baby.* All wrong things to say, but what would have been right?

We persevered, Anna and I, and eventually our coworkers turned attention to other matters and we, for our parts, slipped back into the roles we'd vacated with what I can only describe as gratitude. Brian had been right; we needed the routine, a reason to get up in the morning and shower, a reason to get dressed and out of the house.

If going back to work was the first step in reclaiming our lives, scheduling a vasectomy was the second. Birth control pills were too big of a risk for Anna, now that we knew of the factor V Leiden. No matter what, I vowed, I would never put Anna through such heartache again. We'd lost so much at that point; we'd wasted too much time chasing a dream that had led to nothing but sorrow. I could scarcely remember what life had been before the desire for children overshadowed everything. I wanted Anna back; I wanted our marriage back. I wanted to rid not only our house, but our lives of the ghosts of the children we would never have.

On sleepless nights in my cell, surrounded by the sounds of snoring men and muted footsteps, I often lie awake and ponder the irony of life. I've come to believe the course of our lives is set. We think we're making choices; we delude ourselves into believing we maintain some fragile control over our future, but what if that isn't so?

What if, instead of controlling our own destiny, the universe has decided our fate for us? What if each of us is nothing more than an insignificant cog in the wheel, a tiny particle swept along in some sort of universal plan in which we have no say? What if, no matter what we do, no matter what measures we take to avoid it, our conclusion is predestined? I had vowed to keep Anna safe, to do whatever I could to protect her from a life of pain. How could it be, then, if not for some cosmic irony, that I had killed her?

Chapter 30
Ripley, Tennessee
January 7, 2013: Attorney Consult

"Cross went well today, don't you think?" Brian took the seat across from me. "Your neighbor was clearly a hostile witness for the prosecution. He did a good job of putting your actions into context when given the chance."

I nodded, somewhat wary, unsure of where this was going.

"Our turn is coming, Phillip. Dr. Gillespie will dispute Cathy's testimony regarding your 'violent' behavior towards Anna on the day Jeffrey was born. We have at least a dozen witnesses willing to testify that you and Anna had a strong marriage, by all appearances, and that you expressed nothing but excitement when she became pregnant with Peter."

I nodded again, waiting. I knew from previous meetings with my team of attorneys that the prosecution would work to build their case on the premise that I was a violent man who had sworn, angrily and repeatedly after Jeffrey's death, that I would do whatever it took to keep Anna from having another baby. Their argument, I had been warned, would be that I had been so enraged by Anna becoming pregnant again that I had attempted to kill both Anna and Peter, leaving Anna dead, and Peter gravely disabled.

"Until then," Brian continued, "the prosecution is going to continue to try to paint you as a violent, angry man. I don't want you to let it bother you, and most of all I don't want you to show anger. That would play right into their hands."

"I won't," I said, speaking for the first time. "I'm not angry, Brian." I wasn't, at least not with the prosecutors, or the witnesses. Since my initial outburst during Cathy's testimony I'd managed to compartmentalize my emotions, separating whatever feelings of betrayal I might have originally had from my overwhelming need to be reunited with Peter. I'd do whatever it took to be with my son.

"Good." Brian sat back, scrutinizing me. "It's only going to get harder. Soon, they'll start to call witnesses from the park."

"I know." I could recall all too clearly the shocked faces of those who witnessed Anna's final moments. "But Brian, they didn't see what they think they saw."

"And we'll work to create doubt on cross. I, for one, think we'll succeed. Phillip"—he hesitated—"what really worries me is when it's our turn, when we get to present your defense. You may hear some things that are disturbing."

"What do you mean?" Surely, if I could listen to weeks of testimony describing me as a monster, I could handle anything the defense had to say.

"I mean that in order to save you, we can't save Anna."

"What the hell are you talking about, Brian?"

"I don't think you've been as forthcoming with me as you might have," he said. "I understand your need to protect Anna, Phillip. Hell, I'd like to protect her, too. But we can't. To that end, we'll be bringing forth some witnesses. Her doctor, for one. But also some coworkers, friends from work, people like that."

"Coworkers? Why?"

"They have things to tell us," answered Brian. "She confided in people."

"Brian, I've told you what happened."

"Yes," he said, "to some extent. But you didn't tell me all of it. You didn't tell me about the months leading up to … to the incident. And you didn't tell me about the fights. You said it was an accident. But it wasn't, was it Phillip? You promised me the truth, and now's the time to tell it."

Brian was right; there were things I had not told him. I was torn, I think, between wanting to protect Anna, and struggling to maintain the denial in which I'd lived not only leading up until the moment Peter was born, but also in the first weeks of his life. The Anna I see in my mind is the Anna with masses of curls falling down her back, the Anna whose smile lit up her whole face. I see her laughing, reading, sleeping, hiking. What I don't see—what I refuse to see— is what, in the darkest hours of night, my mind insists I saw that horrible morning.

Chapter 31
Spring, 2007

"Where do you see yourself in five years?" Brian's voice was soft, mellowed by beer. He leaned his head back against the lounge chair, his face barely visible in the moonlight. I tossed another stick onto the fire and sat back to consider my answer.

"It's a pointless question," said Anna as she stretched her bare feet closer to the fire pit and swirled the wine in her glass. "Five years ago, I would have never believed I could enjoy life again. I would have never thought I'd sit at a campfire in the Smoky Mountains with the two of you, drinking beer and philosophizing as if we're still twenty year old students. I thought, back then, that after everything we'd been through, we'd be irrevocably changed, but as it turns out, life has a way of meandering on. Five years from now, who knows? Who cares? Who even thinks about it?"

"Well, now, that's a bit of a pessimistic view, isn't it? Catch your breath, there, Socrates, and tell us what you really think," said Brian, eliciting a laugh from Anna.

"I don't think it's pessimistic at all," she responded. "At least I don't mean for it to be. I just mean, I think we both learned a long time ago"—she glanced at me, as if for validation—"that nothing is certain. Given that, does it even make sense to have five year plans? Or ten year plans? What if you put so much energy into the planning of life that you never get around to the living of life?"

I reached across the space between us to take her hand. "I'll go with Anna on this one," I said. "I'm not sure mapping out a life through a series of plans is such a good idea. What happens if the plan doesn't work? Is life a failure, then?"

Brian took a long swig of beer. "Don't know," he said. "Define failure."

"Well, that's the crux of the whole issue, isn't it?" Anna reached to the picnic table behind us and refilled her glass. "How does one define success? Is it internal, or external? Is it an abstract idea, or something tangible? Take you for example, Brian."

"Oh, Lord," said Brian, throwing an arm over his eyes. "I'm not sure I want to be the example."

"You own a law firm, for heaven's sake. You have plenty of money, you travel whenever and wherever you want. You have tons of friends, and women love you. Are you a success?"

"The argument could be made that I'm a failure at maintaining relationships. A roué. A libertine."

"Could it?" Anna pressed on. "You're quite able to maintain relationships when you want to. Look at us." She gestured to the three of us. "We've been friends for nearly twenty years. Maybe instead of being a failure at relationships, you're a success at avoiding entanglements." She grinned. "It's all in how you frame it."

"Ah," said Brian. "I rather like that."

"I do think it's about reframing," I said, squeezing Anna's hand. "One person's idea of failure might be another person's idea of success."

Anna leaned over to kiss my cheek, nearly toppling her chair in the process. "You're thinking of your father," she said as I righted her, and she was correct; I was.

In some ways, I don't think my father ever got over Jeffrey's death. I know he never understood our desire to move on with our lives, leaving the dream of children behind. Perhaps some of it was generational; he didn't seem able to grasp the idea of family—indeed the *purpose* of family—if that idea didn't include raising children. While Anna and I were able to reframe our idea of family, he demonstrated through both his words and his deeds that I had failed. I don't think this was deliberate on his part; rather, he judged me by his definition of success instead of my own, and I simply failed to meet the standard.

Anna and I had used the years following Jeffrey's death to refocus our energy and attention on our marriage and our careers. That night around the fire, I sincerely thought we had succeeded at both, though I was later to learn otherwise. We were gentle with each other, but I had viewed that as a good thing. We had seen each other's breaking point. We were aware, as many people are not, that our lives existed on shifting sands. Because of that, we held a deep appreciation for not only each other, but for each day. We had made it through the depths of hell, and the other side was heaven by comparison, for the simple fact it wasn't hell. We would not risk the contentment we'd found by longing for something different. Or so I had thought.

I did not have the sort of relationship with my father that would have allowed me to speak with him of such things in a way he might understand. Because of that, the distance that had always existed between us continued during a time circumstances might have served to bring us closer. When I received a phone call summoning me to the hospital a couple of years after Jeffrey's death, it was too late. A drunk driver on a sunny Sunday morning along a straight stretch of I-40 had seen to that. Thankfully, I did have some hours with my mother before she succumbed to her injuries. My father, however was already gone.

Across the fire pit Brian stirred, bringing me back to the present. "What made you ask that, any-way?" I asked him as I reached to catch the beer he tossed my way.

Brian grunted, flipping a bottle cap into the cooler and leaning back on the lounge. "I've got to hire some help at work. Been conducting interviews, and that's one of those questions everyone says you're supposed to ask. In the middle of asking it today, I wondered what the point of it was. Is anyone really going to be honest? I mean, half the kids in there don't know what they're going to eat for lunch, much less what they'll be doing in five years. The other half are too smart to tell me what they *really* think, which is probably along the lines of, 'Anywhere but here, ass-hole.'"

I laughed. "It is a ridiculous question, isn't it? I wonder if anyone ever turns out to be right with their answer. A lot can happen in five years."

If I thought I'd understood that concept on that moonlit night in 2007, I grasped it on an entirely new level when, five years later, I sat in my cell waiting to hear my fate.

Chapter 32
Ripley, Tennessee
January 7, 2013: Attorney Consult

"Phillip? Are you okay?" Brian's voice sounded muffled and distant, as if making its way through buried tunnels to reach me. I shook my head to clear it of images I did not want to see.

"I'm fine. I just … Promise me something, Brian."

Across the table from me he stiffened. "I'm not really in a position to make promises, Phillip," he said. "And you're not really in a position to ask for them."

"True enough," I conceded with a shrug, "but I'm asking anyway. Promise me you won't hurt Anna any more than you have to."

He blew out a breath, clearly frustrated. "In case you've forgotten, Anna is dead."

I flinched at the words. "You know what I mean. Promise you'll protect her memory. She was a good person, a good wife, given everything she went through. Don't betray her now."

He stood and began to pace, a habit of late, hands shoved into his pockets. "My job is to get you out of here," he said. "I think I can do that, but I can't do it if I protect Anna at your expense. This isn't a matter of blaming the victim in order to save the perpetrator, Phillip. Sometimes, the victim is guilty."

"But she wasn't, Brian. She told me. She *begged* me, but I refused to listen. She reached out to me for help, and I let her down in every way possible. Anna's not the guilty party here. I am."

He moved to stand over me, leaning in and forcing me to look at him. "If you believe Anna wasn't guilty," he said, "it's only because you haven't seen Peter. One glance at that baby and there's no doubt of guilt."

I closed my eyes against a wave of pain. "How is Peter?"

"That's something else we need to discuss. He's going home, Phillip. They can't keep him any longer. There hasn't been improvement in a long, long time. He remains in a persistent vegetative state—"

"They don't know that," I snapped. "Remember that case a couple of years ago? The one where they thought the man was in a vegetative state, and he wasn't? He was fully aware, he just couldn't communicate. How do they know that's not the case with Peter? Hell, he's a *baby*, Brian! How would they even *know* if he's in a vegetative state? What's he supposed to do, dance the tango?"

Brian moved to sit across from me again, and this time he was the one struggling to maintain eye contact. "They know, Phillip. He's nearly ten months old. He should be sitting, crawling, interacting, even pulling to stand, but he's not doing any of those things. He's been tested in every way imaginable, multiple times. MRIs, CAT scans, EEGs, blood tests … you name it, and he's had it. He suffered a severe anoxic brain injury, a complete lack of oxygen for what was clearly an extended amount of time. A *deliberately* extended amount of time." He looked meaningfully at me. "He's not aware of anything around him. He doesn't track movement. He doesn't respond to stimuli. He's fed through a tube. Just about the only thing Peter is able to do is to breathe on his own, and even that needs to be monitored. You know these things, Phil. I've told you."

I was suddenly too tired to support my own weight; my head dropped onto the table between us. It was cool against my cheek, and it smelled of salt. I wondered about the parade of men who'd sat at that table, their sweaty hands clasped in—what? Hope? Fear? Anger? Where were they now? And how had I gotten there? If Peter wasn't Peter, if he no longer existed as Peter, what was the point of it all?

"Back to what I was saying, Phillip. Peter is being released."

That got my attention, and I sat up. "Released? To where?"

Brian cleared his throat, rubbing again at the scar on the table he seemed to favor. "To Cathy."

My mouth dropped open. "You can't be serious."

"I know what you're thinking, Phil, and I agree with you. Unfortunately, I had no say in the matter. And Connie will be there; Cathy still lives with her, so at least you'll have the comfort of knowing Anna's mother is overseeing things. And I'll check on him, too, you know I will."

I was flooded with a mixture of both fear and fury. "Cathy? Are they crazy? What, so one sister couldn't ki—" Coming to my senses, I clamped my mouth shut before I could say more, but Brian knew.

"Now we're getting somewhere," he said.

Chapter 33
Winter, 2008

Anna looked beautiful, and I told her so.

"Really?" she asked. "The dress isn't too much?"

I wasn't sure what she meant by *too much*. Cleavage? Never. Curve-hugging fabric? Tantalizing. Deep blue color? Perfect. Which is what I also told her. "You're perfect."

I was rewarded by a kiss—not one of those we've-been-married-for-years little pecks, mind you, but a kiss deep enough and real enough that I was tempted to scrap our fancy night out for a cozy night in. I had not had a kiss like that in some time, and I would have suggested staying in, except that this night was all about Anna, who was the guest of honor.

"Are you nervous?" I asked.

"About the party, no. About the job, a little. But excited, too."

Anna had just been promoted to Dean of Students, a position she'd coveted for years. She was a natural advocate for students, and she already had plans for implementing various activities and policies on their behalf. Though she had never spoken of it, I had always suspected working with students filled a void for Anna. She would not have college-aged children of her own, but engaging and advising the children of others allowed her to experience some of what she would otherwise miss. I said as much to her as she turned to allow me to fasten her necklace.

She seemed startled, even a little angry, by my assessment. "No, Phil. That's not it at all." I looked up from struggling with the tiny clasp to find her eyes in the mirror. She frowned. "You, of all people, should know that."

"I'm sorry, Anna. I didn't mean to upset you. I'm not even sure how I did." Anna and I rarely disagreed; she was much too reticent to derive pleasure from fighting, and after growing up with my opinionated father, I craved a peaceful environment at home. Looking back, I think our reluctance to address issues in a forthright manner is what ultimately led to our end. After all we'd been through we worked hard to protect not only ourselves, but each other. We told each other we'd survived not only intact, but stronger for it, but that wasn't true. Our strength was based on denial, a fragile foundation, to be sure. But those insights were gained during long nights alone in my cell. The night of Anna's party, I was caught off guard by her sudden irritation with me.

"I just can't believe you'd minimize this"—she gestured with her hands—"this whole thing, my promotion, the party, everything, by drawing that conclusion. It's sort of chauvinistic, don't you think? To assume everything I do in life is related to the difficulty we had trying to have children?"

I was too surprised to speak, but Anna forged ahead.

"It's been years, Phil. Years. And believe it or not, not everything I've done since then has been some sad attempt to fill a void. I never even think about it anymore. Do you?"

I did, sometimes, and I told her so. "But not as much as I used to."

"Do you feel as if we're missing something?" she asked, and I thought about it before answering.

"Maybe," I said. "I definitely worry *you* might feel we're missing something."

"Remember what you said about your father? That he used his definition of success when sizing up your life?" I nodded, and she turned to face me. "That's what you're doing now. You're insinuating that I must be unhappy, that I must feel as if I've failed, because we don't have children. But that's not my issue, Phil, it's yours."

I was pelted by the truth of her words. In some secret place, some hidden room of my psyche, I think I did label our lack of children as a failure, not Anna's failure, but mine. Until she verbalized it, I wasn't even aware of my bias, and I don't know if it stemmed from an unconscious internalizing of my father's values, or from the insecurities that had dogged me all my life. I had never felt masculine enough in my father's eyes. I'd never been athletic, or strong, or even particularly brave. Was I really enough of a Neanderthal to equate manhood with procreation? Apparently on some deep level, I was.

"You're right," I told her, "and I'm sorry. Until you said it, I didn't even realize …"

"I know," she said, "and it makes me feel sad for you, that you still feel as if we've missed out on something. But I don't, Phil. I really don't. When I look back at everything we went through, I wish I could go back and tell my younger self to just stop it, already. Why did we put ourselves through that? Why didn't we just accept early on that we were meant to be childless? We had a great marriage, and we have a good marriage now. The worst part of our marriage was when we tried to add to it."

I have to admit, I was a little surprised by the harshness of Anna's statements, but I couldn't help but recognize the truth in them. We did have a good marriage. We both enjoyed our careers, and we had the financial freedom to more or less indulge ourselves at will. Our time was our own, to do with as we pleased; we had always enjoyed each other's company, and we shared the same hobbies. I had no doubt that had we had children, we would have continued to enjoy a good life, albeit a different one—certainly a less self-centered one.

Anna must have read my thoughts, because she moved towards me and wrapped her arms around my waist. "If we'd had children," she said, the anger leaving her voice, "it still would have been a good life, but it wouldn't have been this one, and I like this one just the way it is. I wouldn't change a thing, and it bothers me sometimes that it seems as if you view this life as a consolation prize, as if we lost out on curtain number one and had to settle for curtain number two."

"That's not true, Anna." But wasn't it? Didn't I sometimes see it that way? Anna and I had spent many years building our lives around the idea of when we might have a child. We moved from the city, bought a house with plenty of land, ensured the back-yard had room for a swing set, even remarked on the convenience of our long, paved driveway: *Won't it be great for teaching our kids to ride a bike?* Wasn't it natural, then, to view our life without children as the second choice?

"Enough of this," Anna said, pushing away from me. "We need to get a move on or I'll be late to my own party."

In the early years of our marriage, we had agreed never to end a discussion without reaching a resolution. It was an idealistic goal, a vow made by two young, naïve newlyweds who had no way of knowing each disagreement, each misinterpretation, missed opportunity, or misspoken word left a shadow made of webs, the tendrils reaching through the years to weave a unique tapestry of misunderstandings. What in the beginning had seemed simple—*Are you listening to me? Did you forget to pick up the milk? Do you have to work late again?*—becomes, over time, fraught with nuances and hidden meanings. *Do you still love me? Do you ever think of me? Is this still what we want?*

I understood more from Anna's expression, her quick redirection combined with the stiffening of her shoulders, than I did from her words. It had always been that way with Anna. I had come to learn that the Zen-like calm she projected was capable of masking an astounding depth of emotion.

Once, shortly after we married, I'd come home to find Anna lying across our bed in tears. I can truth-fully say until that point I'd never seen her cry. "What is it?" I'd asked, alarmed, dropping my briefcase in the doorway and rushing to her side.

"You forgot," she said, sitting up to look at me and wiping the tears from her cheeks.

"Forgot? Forgot what?" It wasn't a holiday. It was months away from her birthday or our anniversary. I couldn't imagine what I might have forgotten.

"I told you I wanted to have lunch with you this week. I told you I missed you, with all the hours you're putting in at the lab. You said you'd check your schedule and we'd make a date, but you never did."

I nearly laughed, I was so relieved. "Is that it? I thought something horrible had happened, like someone had been in an accident or something."

"What do you mean, 'Is that it?'" I watched her expression morph from sadness to disbelief.

"But we didn't have a plan, did we? I mean, I got busy at work and I forgot to check my schedule, but it's not as if I stood you up, right?" I was struck by a thought. "Or did I? Did we make a lunch date for today?"

"No, we did not," she said, standing from the bed and moving towards the door, "because my loving husband never made one."

"Anna, come on," I pleaded, caught somewhere between alarm and amusement. "You made a simple statement that you wanted to have lunch sometime. It didn't work out this week, but we can have lunch sometime next week. It's really not that big of a deal, is it?"

"The *deal*," she said, spinning around to face me, "is that you didn't *listen* to me. You didn't *hear* me. I said I wanted to have lunch with you this week, and you blew it off without any consideration for what I was telling you."

I blinked, confused. "But I did hear you," I said.

"So you heard me, but you just didn't care?"

"I …" I truly didn't know what to say to that; there didn't seem to be a way out. "Of course I care," I said, but she interrupted me.

"Really? Well, if you cared, then why didn't you check your schedule like you said you would, so we could make a lunch date?"

"I guess …" I took a moment to try to regroup, unsure how to fix things between us. Anna was still waiting tables at that time, as well as taking some night classes. Her schedule was never set; some mornings I left before she awakened, some nights she was gone when I got home, either at work or in class. There were times we went a day or two without seeing each other. I missed her, of course, but I was working such long hours I probably didn't feel the absence as keenly as she did.

"I guess I didn't realize how important it was to you," I finally said. "I didn't understand that you were making an actual request. I thought you were just saying it would be nice to have lunch sometime, and I agreed with you. It would be nice. It will be nice. I miss you."

Anna was unrelenting. "What I said was, 'I'd like to have lunch with you this week.' What's so hard to understand about that? What do I need to do, jump up and down and yell before you hear me?"

I was struck by how young and vulnerable she looked; I wasn't used to seeing Anna that way. I stood from the bed and moved towards her. "No," I said. "No, you don't have to do that. I'll listen more closely from now on, okay? I'm really sorry, Anna. I would never do anything to hurt you."

"Well, you did," she said, before coming to lean against me, accepting my embrace.

We'd both grown and matured in the passing years, but one thing hadn't changed: Anna still understated her needs, and I still had a difficult time hearing them. We'd learned to compensate, in some ways, or at least I had. I knew now, when Anna expressed displeasure, it ran much deeper than appeared.

We would go to the party, and we would mingle and make small talk. I would refill her drink, laugh at her humor, and place a proprietary hand at the small of her back. She would introduce me to colleagues I had not met, making me sound a much more interesting person than I am. No one would know that underneath the surface of our pleasantries, Anna was still angry while I … well, I had the distinct feeling trouble was brewing.

Chapter 34
Ripley, Tennessee
January 8, 2013: Trial Transcript

Court Clerk: Dr. Williams, would you state your full name for the record, please?

Dr. Williams: Robert Lee Williams.

The Court: You may proceed, Mr. Young.

Prosecutor: Thank you, Your Honor. What is your profession, Dr. Williams?

Dr. Williams: I teach a Tennessee history course at Dyersburg State Community College.

Prosecutor: Do you know the defendant?

Dr. Williams: I know him socially, from events he would attend with his wife.

Prosecutor: So you knew Anna Lewinsky.

Dr. Williams: I did. We were colleagues at Dyersburg State. She started out as an adjunct professor years ago, back in '96 or '97, I believe. At that time, I'd been with the college for several years. I started there in '91. She taught philosophy. She eventually worked her way up, first as full time faculty, and later as Dean of Students.

Prosecutor: Would you categorize Mrs. Lewinsky as a happy person, doctor?

Defense Attorney: Objection. Speculative.

The Court: Sustained. Rephrase the question, Counselor.

Prosecutor: Did Mrs. Lewinsky ever speak to you about her marriage?

Dr. Williams: She did. She spoke often of her husband. Until recently, she seemed very happy in her marriage.

Prosecutor: When did you notice a change, Dr. Williams?

Dr. Williams: Over the last couple of years she was alive. In 2011, 2012 something changed.

Prosecutor: In what way did something change?

Dr. Williams: Before then, she had mentioned her husband the way we all mention our spouses. She might tell us what they'd done the weekend before, or mention he'd gotten a raise or a bonus. You know, just the typical things. Or she'd tell us something funny or endearing he'd said. They seemed like any ordinary couple who'd been married some length of time. Maybe even happier, because they had had so many years to focus on their marriage. I don't mean to offend.

Prosecutor: It's okay, Dr. Williams. Continue please.

Dr. Williams: Well, I mean because they didn't have children, they traveled a great deal. They spent a lot of time together, more than they could have if they'd had children. Anna seemed to enjoy it.

Prosecutor: But in the last couple of years that changed?

Dr. Williams: It did. Anna just didn't seem as happy. She complained about things, which she'd never done before. She mentioned more than once that her husband, Mr. Lewinsky, was stuck in the past. She didn't think he'd ever made peace with the fact they wouldn't have children. She said she felt as if, at some level, he held her responsible.

Prosecutor: Was this something they fought about?

Dr. Williams: I don't know if "fought" is the right word. She would get frustrated. I think it hurt her, feeling as if she weren't enough for her husband.

Defense Attorney: Objection. Witness is speculating.

The Court: Sustained.

Prosecutor: Dr. Williams, what, specifically, did Anna say to you to indicate she felt she wasn't "enough," as you put it, for her husband?

Dr. Williams: She sometimes worried that her husband would rather be with someone younger, someone able to have children.

Prosecutor: I have no further questions for this witness, Your Honor.

The Court: Defense, it's your witness.

Defense Attorney: Thank you, Your Honor. Dr. Williams, you were more than friends with Mrs. Lewinsky, weren't you?

Dr. Williams: I'm not sure what you mean.

Defense Attorney: Didn't you, in fact, engage in an affair with Mrs. Lewinsky during the summer of 2011?

Dr. Williams: No. It wasn't like that.

Defense Attorney: Okay, let me rephrase that. Did you ever have sex with Mrs. Lewinsky?

Dr. Williams: Yes. One time. It was a mistake; we were both vulnerable, my wife had just left me, Anna was unhappy, we comforted—

Defense Attorney: Did you love Mrs. Lewinsky?

Dr. Williams: Well, yes, but—

Defense Attorney: Do you like Mr. Lewinsky, Dr. Williams?

Dr. Williams: Why, I … Not particularly, no.

Defense Attorney: Why is that, Dr. Williams?

Dr. Williams: I'm not sure there is a particular reason, really. I suppose because he seemed to be so out of touch with what Anna needed from him, and I cared for her.

Defense Attorney: Do you have children, Dr. Williams?

Dr. Williams: No. My ex-wife and I were never blessed with children.

Defense Attorney: Were you aware that Mr. Lewinsky had a vasectomy some years ago?

Dr. Williams: Yes. Anna had mentioned it.

Defense Attorney: Curious, isn't it, that Mrs. Lewinsky became pregnant.

Prosecutor: Objection!

The Court: Sustained. Counselor, if you have a question, ask it.

Defense Attorney: Let the record state I'm showing the witness what's been marked as Defendant's Exhibit 'N' for Identification. Dr. Williams, do you recognize this document?

Dr. Williams: Yes.

Defense Attorney: It arrived in my office just this morning. Could you tell the court what it is, exactly?

Dr. Williams: It's a summons.

Defense Attorney: What sort of summons, Dr. Williams?

Dr. Williams: To let … To let Phillip know I've filed a Petition to Establish Paternity of … of Peter. Look, I'm sorry, Mr. Young, Your Honor. I should have said something, I know, but I just … I just need to know.

Defense Attorney: Should Mr. Lewinsky be found guilty of murder and lose custody of his son, that would make this process much easier for you, wouldn't it, Dr. Williams?

Dr. Williams: Well, I suppose, but that's not—

Defense Attorney: I'd ask that Defendant's Exhibit 'N' for Identification be introduced into evidence as Defendant's #18.

The Court: Any objections?

Prosecutor: We would ask for a short recess, Your Honor, and a brief consultation, if possible.

The Court: We will have order in this courtroom! Let's take a fifteen minute recess. Counselors, meet me in my chambers.

Chapter 35
Ripley, Tennessee
January 8, 2013: Attorney Consult

"I'm sorry, Phil. But you know I had to do it."

I'd been surprised, upon my return from the courthouse, to be taken from my cell. I hadn't expected Brian. It had been a harrowing day in court, and I'd looked forward to the dark stillness of my cell.

"Phil?"

I didn't answer him. I was barely capable of holding myself upright in the chair. All I wanted was sleep, that delicious escape.

"You did know, right?"

Knowing and accepting are two very different things, but I didn't have the strength to explain that to Brian. Had I known? Of course. Anna had even tried to confess at one point, but I'd stopped her. Why? Because as I said, knowing and accepting are two very different things.

It is an indisputable fact of life that sometimes the brain knows things the heart chooses not to accept. Signs, nuances, subtleties; the brain picks up on these things, organizing and cataloguing information with astounding efficiency. Given free reign, the information the brain gathers is often enough to break a heart, so we set up firewalls and boundaries to protect it.

"How could they not have known?" we ask of the parents whose child took a gun to school. "She must have known," we say of the wife whose husband has bedded half the women in town. "He can't be that stupid," we say of the grown son whose father extorted millions. "They can't be that blind; they must have known."

What we fail to consider is that sometimes, in the dark of life, denial seems the only route to survival. It's a mirage, of course; the truth will always win in the end. But in the moment, faced with what seems to be insurmountable pain, our heart sometimes decides for us. Had I known on a cognitive level? Yes. Did I accept it on an emotional level? No. And that's what allowed me to live my life uninterrupted. I'd had too many interruptions by that point; I didn't want to face another.

It's easy to sit in judgment from the smug satisfaction of an unchallenged life, but what of those of us whose life experiences have been more complicated?

"She changed," Brian was saying. "For whatever reasons, she changed, didn't she? She wasn't our little Socrates anymore, was she? I had picked up on a certain cynicism, I suppose you could call it, but I guess I just chalked it up to growing older and wiser. Hell, we're all more cynical. But I hadn't realized, until that damned summons arrived and we started digging ... I'm so sorry, Phil. As your attorney, I did what I had to do. As your friend, I ask your forgiveness. As both your attorney and your friend"—he hesitated—"I need to ask you about Peter—"

"No!" At last I found my voice, and my strength, too. I stood, knocking over my chair, and rushed to the door, pounding on it, frantic to leave that room, and Brian's questions, behind.

Brian and the guard reached me at the same time, Brian placing a hand on my shoulder and squeezing, the guard yanking my arms behind my back and cuffing me. Of the two touches, I most appreciated the guard's.

Chapter 36
Summer, 2011

Anna had been distant. I had first begun to notice it back in the spring. Over the years, at Anna's urging, we'd made a ritual of spending her spring break planning our summer flower garden. It was different every year, both in content and design, and Anna had become somewhat of a local celebrity because of it. Her job was to design and maintain; mine was to build.

Some years, she designed cobbled walkways and tiny goldfish ponds among the flowers. Other years, she fancied tiered designs of exploding colors and textures. One memorable year she planted our initials in flowers of white, surrounding them in a heart-shaped landscape of red. I think she enjoyed challenging herself as much as she enjoyed the compliments from friends and neighbors. For my part I enjoyed the physical labor, the sun hot on my back, the tiller unwieldy in my hands, nearly as much as I anticipated Anna's creative designs.

But that spring, as the date of her break from school arrived, Anna said nothing of our garden. When I mentioned it to her, she shrugged. "I don't know, Phil. Maybe it's time to do something different. It seems silly after a while, doesn't it? All that time and energy spent on something that lasts such a short amount of time."

I was puzzled by her attitude, which seemed very unlike Anna. But then again, Anna had seemed very unlike Anna for quite some time. She had always been a quiet person, reserved, self-contained. But for the past few months, her inherently quiet nature had become something else. Something darker.

Anna had sunk into a deep depression after losing Jeffrey; she came through that experience changed. No doubt we both did. But though Anna would never have admitted it, I knew she had flirted with depression more than once since that time. There were periods, thankfully few and far between, during which I could see she struggled. She grew quiet, withdrawn, even somewhat detached. From the outside looking in, those later bouts of depression paled in comparison to what she had experienced when Jeffrey died; still, it was enough to cause me concern throughout the latter part of our marriage.

For years I had assumed the residual sadness lurking underneath the surface of Anna's outward presentation was directly related to Jeffrey's death. When asked, however, Anna had made it clear she had emotionally moved on, putting our painful past behind her. She'd even expressed anger towards me for having thought otherwise, and she'd resented the assumptions I had made.

I was careful after that, never mentioning her darker moods but taking care to be gentle with her when I sensed she might be struggling. Her periodic bouts of sadness might not have been the direct result of Jeffrey's death, but I did believe his passing had been a catalyst of sorts, a triggering mechanism that uncovered a part of Anna neither of us had previously known existed, perhaps a part connected to the colorful ancestors she'd tentatively mentioned to me years before.

And maybe a part of me, no stranger to melancholy, found comfort in Anna's forays into my familiar land. Not consciously, of course—never consciously. Still … was I too quick to accept her quieter moments? Did I derive some sense of purpose in bravely shoring her up? Was I relieved, on some level, that I wasn't the only one who could at times seem moody? A man has plenty of time to ponder things when he sits for hours alone in a cell. The questions and self-recriminations come easily; the answers are more elusive.

At any rate, I wondered that spring if Anna was again sinking into another depression. As spring passed into summer and summer to autumn, I watched her pull further into herself and further away from me. There were long silences between us, silences I didn't know how to breach. She spent a great deal of time at school those months, complaining of paperwork and meetings while at the same time seeming eager to leave our home, which had suddenly become an uncomfortable place for her to be.

We were rarely intimate, a fact I chalked up to our age, our history, and the comfortable knowledge that we were together for the long haul. We had all the time in the world, or so I'd believed. Anna's thoughts, I later learned, were somewhat different.

I remember it not as if it were yesterday, but as if it were mere seconds ago. We were getting ready for work, jockeying for space in the bathroom as we'd always done, I brushing my teeth and Anna wrapped in a towel, smoothing moisturizer into her arms.

Her towel slipped and she grabbed for it, but not quickly enough. It landed at her feet and I reached to retrieve it, thinking nothing of it, until I straightened to see her, naked. I realized then how long it had been since I'd seen Anna in the light, unclothed. I also realized—and I saw by her expression that she knew I had—that Anna was pregnant.

Chapter 37
Lauderdale County Jail
January 8, 2013

My Dearest Peter,

As I write this you're sleeping, if your schedule is as it should be. You're a growing boy; you need your rest. And if the universe is kind, as it sometimes is, you're dreaming of ballgames, water-balloon fights, bicycle rides and best friends.

But do you even know what these things are?

Forgive me, my son. News of your condition comes to me second-, third-, or even fourth-hand. None of it is encouraging, and all of it frightens me.

Here's what you should know. Your mother loved you. I loved you. You were a dream come true for us, a dream two decades in the making.

That's a big burden for a little boy; don't think I don't know that. It is through no fault of your own that my dream and your mother's dream somehow diverged through the years. If you dig to the heart of the matter, the reason for the heartbreak, it's only that we didn't find you sooner; that's how important you were to both of us. You, I believed, were to be the answer to all of our prayers.

For that, I apologize. It was unfair of me to place such a burden on your tiny shoulders. Had I listened to your mother, had I done as she asked—begged—you would not be suffering so. No matter what happens, should you grow up to read, explore the internet, watch old crime shows, or whatnot, know this: No matter what you read, no matter what you hear, no matter what they say, your mother loved you just as much as I do. She did, Peter. She did.

When one has spent the better part of one's life wishing for something—for someone—and that something—or someone—suddenly appears, even if in an unexpected way, it's still a dream come true.

It is, Peter, and don't ever let anyone tell you otherwise.

You were my dream come true.

You are my dream come true.

I love you, son. And so did your mother.

Forever and always,
Dad

Chapter 38
Summer, 2011

"Phil—"

"Stop." I held my hand up as if to physically ward off Anna's words. Instinct, an innate sense of self-preservation warned me; I knew I could not hear whatever it was she was about to say.

"But I—"

"No, Anna." I shook my head and turned away from her.

I convinced myself at that moment the baby was mine. I willed the seed of that belief to grow. After all, some tiny percentage of vasectomies fail. It hardly mattered to me that the number was so small as to be nearly nonexistent. Nor did it matter that I could scarcely remember the last time Anna and I had engaged in any sort of activity that might lead to pregnancy.

What mattered was that as I stood there looking at Anna, who held the towel against her swollen front as if to hide herself from me, I didn't see the unhappy, middle-aged woman she had become. I didn't see the short-cropped hair, faded of its color, or the extra ten pounds, or the downward lines around her mouth.

I saw a beautiful young woman laughing on a balmy fall night. I smelled the crisp scent of the river and heard the distant horn of a barge. I was mesmerized, the wind blowing curls across her face as my heart stuttered. It had taken all my willpower not to wind my fingers through that hair and pull her up against me.

Intertwined with that image, superimposed upon it, was that of a devastated young mother bent forward in agony, holding the still form of her infant son against her breast and looking into my eyes as we both began a descent into hell from which we would never fully recover.

"Do you want a divorce?" I asked, the question squeezing past the barriers I was already erecting against the knowledge in my mind.

"No." She shook her head, tears spilling down her cheeks. "Oh, Phil, I—"

"Do you love me?" I asked, because it suddenly mattered terribly.

"Always," she said, stepping towards me. "I always have, Phil. I always will. This was noth—"

"Hush, Anna. Don't say it."

She buried her face in the towel and began to cry. "I just couldn't ... sometimes it's so *dark* here, Phil. Every time I manage to pull myself out of it to move on, you pull me back. You won't let it go; you define everything by Jeffrey, and I can't live that way. It's hard enough—"

"Stop it!" I slammed my palm down on the sink vanity and Anna jumped, once again losing possession of her towel. "We won't do that, Anna. Neither of us is without guilt. We won't stand here and point fingers. It's not my place to do that, and it certainly isn't yours."

A case would later be made that my anger regarding Anna's pregnancy propelled me to plan her death, but although that made a neat and tidy package for the jury, it wasn't true. No sooner had my anger surfaced than it dispersed. It was possible, I discovered in that instant, to have such a mix of feelings one ends up feeling nothing at all, much like a fuse that overheats and is subsequently blown. It was an emptiness that proved to be fertile ground for denial.

The only thing I was sure of as I once again retrieved Anna's towel from the floor was that against all reason, I wanted that baby. I *deserved* that baby, by God, not only to make up for all of our past losses, but to make up for the current one, too, the one I steadfastly refused to see. Over the years, I'd accepted the life we had, but the universe was extending another chance to live the life I'd *thought* we'd have. No doubt I was irrational, but it wasn't a violent break with rationality; it was instead a protective one. I wanted to protect what I had: my marriage, my life, my home. And now, my child.

As I handed the towel to her once again, I already envisioned a future much as I'd envisioned two decades before, one with me, Anna, and a baby. In spite of my vasectomy, our prayers were suddenly answered, as if it were meant to be. Providence, fate, whatever was at work I was convinced this time everything would turn out right. Any doubts I had about the origin of the baby were quickly dismissed, neatly excised from the truth that was evident, and instead sealed tightly behind the truth I wanted.

"You'll need an appointment," I said, surprised at my ability to form a coherent sentence out of the jumble in my head.

Anna nodded, her expression a mix of confusion and surprise. "I've already made one for next week," she said, attempting to scrub the tears from her cheeks. "I had hoped … Phil, I'm so *sorry*. As horrible as it sounds, as horrible as this makes me, I had hoped to have it taken care of before you even knew. It's a terrible mistake; I haven't been myself. I just want to erase it all, pretend nothing's changed, go back to what we had …"

Her words swirled around me, some floating into the space between us, others lodging themselves into the cracks of my heart. "What do you mean, 'taken care of?' You can't just erase a *person*, Anna. How could you even have considered such a thing?" I was stunned at her misunderstanding. Of all the revelations I'd had about Anna that morning, this one shocked me the most. For the first time ever, I saw her as someone distinctly different from the person I had married. But then, I was different, too.

"Phil, we obviously can't move forward with this," she glanced down at her front, her eyes huge, her expression disbelieving. "It's not … Phil, *please!* Don't make me say these things. I can't have a baby now. I'm too old; it's too late." Her voice rose. "There are the medical issues; I can't go through that again. This is crazy. All of it is crazy. I can't believe this is happening. Oh, God. I'm so sorry." She folded to the floor, hugging her knees to her chest, her cries muffled by the towel.

The prosecutor would later claim I'd insisted Anna carry the pregnancy to term as a form of punishment. Knowing her medical history, the risks involved, he would insist I'd hoped for the worst, a passive sort of murder, and when that hadn't happened, I'd taken a more aggressive approach. During the months since her death, I'd spent many hours going over things in my mind, questioning my motivations, and I don't believe those accusations to be accurate, not even on a subconscious level. What *was* true, however, was that in the list of things I'd determined to protect, I'd forgotten to include Anna.

So I left her there, rocking against the unyielding oak of the bathroom cabinet.

Chapter 39
Ripley, Tennessee
February 11, 2013: Trial Transcript

Court Clerk: State your full name for the record, please.

Connie Tyler: Connie Jeanette Tyler

Court Clerk: Spell your middle name, please.

Connie Tyler: J-e-a-n-e-t-t-e.

The Court: Mr. Young, you may proceed.

Prosecutor: Thank you, Your Honor. Mrs. Tyler, you are the mother of the victim, is that correct?

Connie Tyler: Yes.

Prosecutor: We're sorry for your loss, ma'am.

Connie Tyler: Thank you.

Prosecutor: Kleenex?

Connie Tyler: Yes. Thank you.

Prosecutor: Mrs. Tyler, when did you learn your daughter was pregnant with her latest child, Peter?

Connie Tyler: Oh, I think it was in October.

Prosecutor: Of 2011, you mean?

Connie Tyler: Yes. That's right.

Prosecutor: Who told you she was pregnant, Mrs. Tyler?

Connie Tyler: Anna did. I knew something was bothering her. She didn't seem well. Sad. Quiet.

Prosecutor: What did she tell you regarding the circumstances of her pregnancy, Mrs. Tyler?

Connie Tyler: I'm not sure what you mean.

Prosecutor: Did she tell you Phillip Lewinsky was not the father of the child?

Connie Tyler: I don't know why you need to do this to her. To her memory. What does it matter now?

Prosecutor: I do apologize, Mrs. Tyler, but I assure you it is important. We all want to see justice done for your daughter. So I need to ask again: Did she tell you Phillip Lewinsky was not the father of her child?

Connie Tyler: What you people don't seem to understand is that sometimes there just isn't any justice. But if you must know, yes. She did. She confided in me one Sunday, when they'd come to our house for dinner. She was highly upset. Crying. I knew something was wrong, so when Phillip and her father retired to the living room, I asked her what was bothering her. She said she was pregnant. I'll be honest with you; I was worried. Because of her history, you know. And even without her history, she was on the older side to be finding herself pregnant. I was afraid for her health.

Prosecutor: And was it at that time she told you Mr. Lewinsky was not the father?

Connie Tyler: Yes.

Prosecutor: I'm sorry, Mrs. Tyler. You're going to have to speak a little louder.

Cathy Tyler: Yes. That's when she told me. It was hard for her to confide in me, and I swore I'd never tell anyone. And now here you are making me.

Prosecutor: Did she say whether or not Mr. Lewinsky was aware of the paternity of the baby?

Connie Tyler: She said she thought he probably knew, but that he wouldn't allow her to talk about it.

Prosecutor: Did she indicate she'd tried to talk to him about it?

Connie Tyler: Yes. She said she'd tried, but he refused to discuss it.

Prosecutor: Mrs. Tyler, did your daughter indicate her feelings about her pregnancy?

Connie Tyler: She said she was worried. She was worried about her health, because of her medical condition and her age. She was also worried about … about losing the baby. About what that would do to her, mentally, you know, after all she'd experienced.

Prosecutor: Mrs. Tyler, I know this is difficult, but did your daughter speak to you about the possibility of an abortion?

Connie Tyler: It was too late for an abortion by the time she told me about the pregnancy, but she did say she had considered it. She said Phillip wouldn't hear of it. She said he flat-out refused to consider abortion.

Prosecutor: Even in spite of the risks to Anna's health, he wouldn't consider abortion?

Connie Tyler: That's what she said.

Prosecutor: Were you also worried about Anna's health?

Connie Tyler: Of course. But she was under the strict supervision of her doctor throughout the pregnancy.

Prosecutor: Mrs. Tyler, after the baby was born, did Mr. Lewinsky ask you to move into his home to help?

Connie Tyler: No. He didn't ask me; I volunteered.

Prosecutor: Didn't he, in fact, tell you he was "at the end of his rope" with Anna and the baby?

Connie Tyler: Yes, but that was because—

Prosecutor: Thank you, Mrs. Tyler. No further questions.

The Court: Mr. Stone? Your witness.

Defense Attorney: Mrs. Tyler, first of all, I'm sorry for your loss.

Connie Tyler: Thank you, Brian. I know you are. Could I have a tissue, please?

Defense Attorney: We would ask the Court for a short recess in order to allow Mrs. Tyler some time to compose herself.

The Court: Granted, Mr. Stone. We'll reconvene in fifteen minutes.

Chapter 40
March 30, 2012

Only once, during all that time, did Anna directly express her wishes, and that was the night of my discovery. We'd not spoken since that morning, since I'd left Anna huddled in the bathroom floor. I'd come home later than usual, having stopped with coworkers for a drink after work, something I rarely did. To be honest, I was a coward. I was afraid to go home. I didn't know what to expect, so I put it off as long as I reasonably could.

To my surprise, I'd arrived home to find it lit with candles, soft music in the background, lasagna, fragrant and steaming, on the table. Anna uncorked the wine just as I walked through the door. I accepted the offered glass willingly and without question, until Anna poured her own glass to the brim and clinked it against mine.

"You're drinking?" I was surprised. In the early years, through the failed pregnancies, all the way through losing Jeffrey, Anna hadn't touched a drop of alcohol, or caffeine either, for that matter. Personally,

I hadn't thought an occasional glass of wine would cause any harm, but Anna had been adamant, rigidly adhering to the dietary advice of her doctors.

But not that night.

"I can drink," she said, "because I'm not keeping this baby. I already told you I have an appointment for next week."

Those were the words that had kept me from home, that had compelled me to spend the evening in a bar instead of with my newly pregnant wife. I'd worked so hard all day to fortify my belief that first, the baby was most certainly mine (of course it was—how could I have even doubted?) and second, we were getting a final chance at a dream we both had shared, that I couldn't bear the thought Anna might be in a very different state of mind. Carefully, I set my glass down and turned to look at her.

"You can't be serious."

"I am, Phil. I'm not a young woman; it's not as if we're still in our thirties, trying to have a family. That life is gone. I'm forty-four years old, too old to have a baby."

"You make it sound as if we're days away from being sent to an old folks' home. Plenty of people have babies at our age, Anna."

"Good for them," she said, and took a long sip of her wine. "But I don't want to. I don't want the anxiety, the worry, the sickness or discomfort. I don't want the mood swings, the depression, the risks involved. I'm too old to be a PTA mom, and I don't have the energy to host slumber parties. Twenty years ago, hell, even ten years ago, I would have jumped at the chance. But I'm too old now, Phil. I don't want it." She shrugged, a gesture I read as a challenge.

"But you're just talking about the abstract idea," I pointed out. "Think of the baby. I think you're letting your fear get in the way of the reality of us finally having a family. This is what we've always wanted."

"No, it isn't." She set her glass down, too, and leaned across the table towards me. "It's what *you've* always wanted. I stopped wanting it a long time ago, when I realized the two of us *are* a family. If you ever listened to me, you'd know that. A baby is the very *last* thing we need."

"You don't mean that, Anna."

"Oh, my God. You …" She shoved her chair back from the table, clearly frustrated. "What does it take for you to hear me? I do mean it, Phil. I'm not in a place to want to raise children. I'm comfortable with my life, my job. Call me selfish, if you need to, but I don't want to give up what I have. It's too late for me to make the changes I'd need to make to raise a child. I've told you that for years. This dinner … This is about working on us, our marriage.

"We have things to work on, Phil. Otherwise, we wouldn't find ourselves in this spot. And I want to do that, to work on things. I love you. I miss you. I think back to our earlier years, even some not-so-early years, and I feel like we've lost ourselves, or maybe it's just me. Maybe *I'm* lost. I've made mistakes, God knows I have, but I want to fix them. A baby won't do that for us. In fact, it's the worst thing that could have happened, and I suppose it serves me right."

We regarded each other across the dining room table, the lasagna congealing in front of us. "Anna," I paused, unsure what to say. "I want to work on our marriage, too, but this isn't going to just … just *go away*, you know."

She shoved aside her plate, folded her hands on the table in front of her. I'd never seen Anna look the way she did that night. She wasn't just determined, she was hard, angry. "It can," she said, with a tilt of her head, "if we make it."

I was shaking my head before she'd even finished. "We just can't do that, Anna. After all we've been through, after all *you've* been through, you'd really be okay with that? Don't you feel that would be like"—I struggled for words—"like slapping karma in the face? Okay, so it's later than we'd planned, but now that it's happened, would you really be okay with …" I couldn't even say the word. "With ending it?"

She crossed her arms and leaned back, her expression defiant. "Are you going to fight me on this? Because if this is some sort of punishment—"

"No." I stopped her before she could say more. "Wait. Let's just slow down. This is so sudden and unexpected for both of us. Let's take some time and think about things, at least a day or two, so we don't make any decisions we'll regret." I was terrified of her words, our words. I knew the things we said that night would set the path for our future, and that frightened me; I wanted to tread very carefully.

"There are so many opportunities for regret here, Anna. I don't want that. I want to fix things, too. You've always been the most important part of my life. I'm not sure where I've failed you, but I'm willing to take a look at it and try to fix things. But we need to be careful here, tonight, with what we say and do. We owe that to each other. Okay?"

As quickly as Anna's anger had appeared, it disappeared, and she dissolved into tears. "It's too late, Phil." I watched helplessly as she wiped her eyes on her shirttail and poured herself another glass of wine. "It's already too late. Either way, we lose; there's simply no good option."

"It's never too late," I told her, "as long as we're both willing to try."

But I had been wrong, and Anna had been right. It was already too late.

We didn't fight again, not after that first day. We'd spent so many years treating each other with kid gloves by that point, I'm not sure either of us knew a way out of it. We arose the next morning almost as if the previous day had never happened. Anna's eyes were swollen from crying and her face was drawn, but her voice was cheerful as she wished me good morning, and she hummed as she cleared away the dinner dishes we'd been too tired to wash the night before.

I watched her carefully, taking my lead from her. If she was willing to move ahead without revisiting our previous discussion, I was only too happy to oblige. She held me close before I left for work, and I returned the embrace, stroking her back for a moment before releasing her.

If her good cheer was too deliberate, I chose not to notice, and when she called later in the day to tell me she loved me I chatted happily with her about any number of mundane topics: the weather, an irritating coworker, a lab test I was running, a quarrelsome student she had to advise. I couldn't remember the last time we had stopped in the middle of a busy day to reach out to one another, and I savored the experience.

Neither of us mentioned Anna's upcoming appointment, and the week passed like any other. I was grateful for that, as well as for Anna's seeming acceptance of her pregnancy. She made an appointment with her doctor, replaced her morning coffee with juice, and the half bottle of wine leftover from our disastrous dinner found its way to the garbage bin, the remaining contents poured down the drain.

Eventually, over time, we shared the news with family and friends, all of whom expressed pleasure once they'd absorbed the initial shock. Unlike with her previous pregnancies, Anna experienced no morning sickness with Peter. She was instead the picture of health. Her condition carefully monitored, she was full of energy and what appeared, to the outside world, anyway, to be if not exactly excitement, at least a cautious acceptance of the upcoming birth.

Only I knew otherwise. Some nights, across the expanse of our bed, I could hear Anna crying. "I can't do this again, Phil," she would say. "It's too late."

I'd shush her, reaching across the darkness to assure her everything would be okay; I truly believed it would. "We'll be fine, Anna," I'd tell her. "You'll see."

"But this isn't what I want. It doesn't feel right; it scares me."

"Anna." I stroked her hair. "We're in this together. We can do this. It'll be fine, more than fine. It'll be wonderful. You'll see."

Looking back, it's almost as if my stark denial of our situation was my lifeline through it all. As long as I could focus on the end result—a baby, *our* baby—I could be okay. I didn't deliberately leave Anna out of that equation; instead, she chose not to join it, and I chose not to change it.

Peter Michael Lewinsky was born at 1:30 a.m. March 30, 2012. My first inclination is to say the birth was relatively easy for Anna, but that's not entirely true. Her labor was relatively fast, as it had been with Jeffrey. Unlike Jeffrey, both Peter and Anna had been monitored closely throughout the pregnancy and delivery, factor V Leiden never far from our thoughts. As a result, Peter entered safely into the world and was placed without incident into Anna's arms.

I suppose it should not have been a surprise to me, given Anna's state of mind throughout the pregnancy, that she exhibited more trepidation than joy upon his arrival. "Do you remember when Jeffrey was born," she asked me, shortly after our friends and families had finally departed for the night, "and they whisked him away? You didn't know where to go, whether to stay with me, or to go with him."

"Of course I remember." I bent to kiss her forehead, stroking a finger along Peter's downy scalp, laughing as he scrunched up his little red face. He already had a head full of Anna's auburn hair, a fact that pleased me. "But you don't have to worry, Anna. Peter is fine. You're fine. We knew this time."

"Do you remember what I said to you?" she asked.

"No," I said. "But let's not think about that now, okay? Let's just enjoy this moment."

"This is important, Phil." She reached across Peter, who nuzzled at her breast, to put a hand on my arm. "Do you remember?"

I didn't. What little I remembered of that night was cloaked in shadows, which is exactly the way I wanted to leave it, and I told her so.

"As the doctor explained what had happened, I could see you were torn," she said. "You didn't know which of us to be with. I told you to go. I said, 'You have to be there for him, because I can't.'"

"Okay," I said, giving in. "But what does this have to do with now?" I was becoming annoyed. I wanted to focus on Peter, count his toes for the umpteenth time and argue over who he most resembled. I wanted to focus on the present; I didn't want to be caught in the past.

"Everything," she answered. "No matter what, you have to be there for Peter if I can't. He will always need one of us to be there."

That drew me up short, jarring me from my irritation. "Are you feeling okay?" I leaned back to better see her face. Her color was good, but her words worried me. I was suddenly terrified of losing her to a stroke. She was on anticoagulants and hooked up to all sorts of medical equipment; none of the beeps or hisses seemed out of sorts with what I'd grown used to, but knowing Anna as I did, I knew I'd need to pay close attention. "I'll get the nurse."

"No, Phil. I'm fine. I feel fine. I just need to know that no matter what, if I can't be there for Peter, you will."

"Of course," I said, my concern mixing with confusion. "But Anna, you don't need to worry. The doctors—"

"Just promise me, Phil. That's all I ask." Her voice was quiet; she sounded drained. I studied her more closely, taking in the fine lines around her eyes, the downward curve of her mouth.

"I promise, honey. I'm here for both of you, no matter what." She leaned her head against the pillow, seemingly satisfied with my answer. "Let me take the baby," I said, reaching for him. "You must be exhausted. Sleep, and I'll take care of Peter."

She handed him over without protest and I gathered him against my chest, enjoying the warm weight of him as I reached to pull the curtains closed before settling into the room's single chair, perfectly content to hold him through the night while Anna slept.

At that time, given her health issues, I'd assumed Anna meant physically—if she couldn't physically be there for Peter. But since that time, I've wondered. What did Anna see? What did she sense? Did she know even then, before Peter had even been bathed, the vernix still evident on his tiny body, that in fact she wouldn't be there for him?

I think she did, and it's this knowledge I hold close to me when doubts creep in, when I see that awful morning in my memory. Anna loved Peter. I believe that, and I believe she knew, and she tried to warn me and to protect him. But I didn't hear her.

Chapter 41
Ripley, Tennessee
February 11, 2013: Trial Transcript

The Court: Your witness has already been sworn in, and you may proceed, Counselor.

Defense Attorney: Thank you, Your Honor. Mrs. Tyler, you've known Phil Lewinsky for many years, haven't you?

Connie Tyler: I have. Over twenty. Just about the same amount of time I've known you.

Defense Attorney: And in all that time, did you ever witness him behaving aggressively towards your daughter Anna?

Connie Tyler: No. Never.

Defense Attorney: Did you ever witness him behaving in a hostile manner towards Anna?

Connie Tyler: No. I never did.

Defense Attorney: Did you have occasion to witness Phil and Anna together during Anna's latest pregnancy?

Connie Tyler: Oh, sure. At least weekly. Sometimes more often. Either they were at our house, or we were at theirs. Or we met out in public, like at church or whatnot.

Defense Attorney: During those visits, how did Phillip treat Anna?

Connie Tyler: The same as always. He was always thoughtful with her. Patient. Caring. Worried about her health, making sure she was comfortable.

Defense Attorney: And after the pregnancy, when you volunteered to move in with Phillip and Anna. Why was that, Mrs.Tyler?

Connie Tyler: Anna was having some trouble adjusting. She was worn out, just plain exhausted. They both were, really. Peter was a little colicky back then. But you know, it's hard on a woman, having a baby. Well, I reckon she was depressed. She wasn't herself, and I could see Phillip needed some help. He couldn't do it all on his own.

Defense Attorney: Even during that time, with both Phillip and Anna exhausted, did you ever see Phillip lose his temper or behave aggressively towards Anna?

Connie Tyler: No. He was worried about her, of course, but he was never angry with her.

Defense Attorney: How about towards the baby? Did he lose his temper with the baby?

Connie Tyler: Oh, not at all. He loves that baby. Phillip is an excellent father.

Defense Attorney: Thank you, Mrs. Tyler. No further questions.

Connie Tyler: Thank you, Brian.

Chapter 42
Spring, 2012

"How is she doing, Phil?" Mrs. Tyler had pulled me aside shortly after dinner, peeking around the doorframe to ensure Anna remained seated in the living room with her father. "She's so quiet."

I shrugged. "Tired, but I guess that's to be expected. We're both tired. Peter was up most of the night last night. The doctor thinks he's a little colicky."

"Poor baby," she said. "I used to put a drop of Caro syrup in Cathy's bottle when she got that way. My mother swore it worked, and it did seem to. Have you tried that?"

I smiled at Mrs. Tyler's home remedy. "We got a prescription for some drops we'll use next time he's fed," I assured her, checking my watch. "Which should be any minute now, as soon as he wakes up. The little rascal keeps us up all night, then wants to sleep all day."

"Well," she said, patting my arm, "if it's any comfort to you, Cathy outgrew it by three months." She peered closer at my face. "But I guess three months can seem like a very long time if you aren't getting any sleep. I do seem to remember being nearly out of my mind with exhaustion, up all night with Cathy, then having to get up and run around after a toddler all day. It wasn't easy, that's for sure."

"It gets a little rough," I agreed. "We're taking turns with him. I try to give Anna a little extra time to sleep because I seem to function better tired than she does."

"Is she really all right, Phil? She's been so quiet lately. She hardly talks at all, not even when I ask her things about the baby."

I wasn't sure how to answer her. Anna *was* quiet, but she was also, if the way I felt was any indication, tired enough to sleep sitting up with her eyes open. But it was more complicated than that. Anna wasn't *Anna*, and hadn't been for a long time. She had said things, expressed feelings lately that concerned me greatly. I was tempted to confide in Mrs. Tyler, but at the same time didn't want to risk upsetting Anna.

She apparently picked up on my hesitation because she pulled me farther into the dark hallway. "What is it, Phil? Something's wrong, isn't it?"

I weighed my words carefully. "She's not happy," I finally told her. "I know it's normal for new mothers to get the baby blues, but this is more than that. I'm worried about her."

"What's she done that's worrying you so?" Her voice was barely more than a whisper.

"She says things, sometimes. Irrational things." I ran my hand through my hair, agitated, unsure how much to admit.

"Like what? Tell me, Phil." She prodded me towards the door to Anna's old room, leading me inside and silently pushing the door closed. "Sit down, hon."

She motioned towards the bed. "Tell me what's going on."

"Sometimes she says things about herself." I took a deep breath. "Things like we'd have been better off if she'd died during the delivery."

Beside me Anna's mother gasped, covering her mouth with one hand. I plunged ahead, relieved to be sharing this with someone who loved Anna as much as I did.

"Other times, she talks about the baby. About how she wants to save him"—I glanced at her, forcing the words out—"from her. She says she needs to save the baby from the life he'll have with her as his mother. She says she thinks your family is cursed."

"What on earth!" Her face had drained of color.

"I know. She told me years ago about relatives living somewhere back in the mountains, people with a criminal history. I just took it as one of those stories all families have, one that probably grows bigger as it gets passed down.

"But lately"—I threw my hands up, overcome by how powerless I felt—"it's all she talks about. She thinks some sort of insanity, a 'bad gene,' she calls it, runs through your family. She's obsessed with it. She thinks she's inherited this gene, and she's convinced Peter has, too. It's gotten to the point that I'm afraid, sometimes, to leave her alone. I don't think she'd do anything, not to herself and certainly not to Peter, but still. I can't take that chance."

"Have you told her doctor what's going on?"

"I did, and he immediately scheduled an appointment, but she refused to let me go in with her, and when she came out she was smiling and joking as if nothing were wrong. I think she convinced him I was overreacting. Or maybe she really thought she was over the worst of it, but she's not. Not by a long shot. I've requested a meeting with him next week. He's told me he can't give me any information without violating Anna's privacy, but he's assured me he'll take into consideration everything I share with him. But if Anna refuses to admit it, what can we do? Mrs. Tyler, I'm at the end of my rope. I just don't know what to do." To my embarrassment, my voice cracked. I truly was at the end of my rope.

Mrs. Tyler leaned over and embraced me. "I'm going to move in with you," she said, and the relief I felt was a physical sensation. "Just until she's feeling back to herself." She let go of me and reached for a Kleenex from the box on the nightstand, dabbing at her eyes.

"She's not completely wrong, you know." She blew her nose before continuing. "There is a history of *something*; I don't know what you'd call it. Maybe it is a bad gene. A couple of generations back. I had always thought that was just the way of people, isolated like they were in the mountains back then. But Cathy." She stopped, looked hard at me. "Don't think I don't know, Phil. Cathy has her faults. She was never easy. I love her, by God, just as much as I love Anna. But I'm not blind. Or stupid."

"But you never saw anything with Anna?" I asked. I had to know; it was inconceivable to me that a woman I'd always considered to be the most level-headed, centered person I'd known was suddenly thrown so off balance.

"No. Never. Anna was always the calm one. Did whatever we asked, never gave us a moment's trouble. But remember I told you I had a case of the baby blues myself." She laughed, a harsh sound. "Baby blues. That's what they called it, you know. Such a cute sounding name. But there wasn't anything cute about it, I tell you. And you couldn't talk about it, not back then. Probably not now, either. You're supposed to be happy, on top of the world; that's what everyone expects. You don't want to let them down, and you don't want to have to put up with the looks people give you if you complain. It's probably even worse for Anna because she was so torn about being pregnant at this point, with her age, and … and everything. My poor little girl."

She patted my leg and stood. "Now let me go give my girl a hug. Then I'm going to pack my bags and make myself at home at your place."

For the first time in weeks, I felt hopeful.

Chapter 43
Ripley, Tennessee
March 4, 2013: Trial Transcript

Court Clerk: Mr. Harris, would you state your name for the record, please?

Joshua Harris: Joshua Eugene Harris.

Court Clerk: Spell your middle name, please.

Joshua Harris: E-u-g-e-n-e.

The Court: Your witness, Mr. Young.

Prosecutor: Thank you, Your Honor. Mr. Harris, you work at the Brownsville Express convenience store on Anderson Avenue in Brownsville, is that correct?

Joshua Harris: Yep.

Prosecutor: What is your job at the store, Mr. Harris?

Joshua Harris: If I'm by myself, I do whatever needs doing. If there's more than one of us there, I take the register.

Prosecutor: Were you working the register the morning of June 3, 2012?

Joshua Harris: I was. Glenda, the other person working, was doing stuff back in the back.

Prosecutor: Mr. Harris, did you have occasion to see the defendant, Mr. Lewinsky, at the Brownsville Express that morning?

Joshua Harris: Sure did. Him and his wife, and the baby, too.

Prosecutor: What time was that?

Joshua Harris: It was 8:15 on the dot. I only know that because I was wondering what was taking Glenda so long in the back. I needed a bathroom break and I couldn't take it until she got back up front.

Prosecutor: Glenda is your coworker?

Joshua Harris: Yeah. She's pretty good, but she's slow.

Prosecutor: What did you see that morning, Mr. Harris?

Joshua Harris: I seen him—the defendant, there— pull up at the pump. Seen him get out, go around back to get the baby. I thought that was kind of weird, him holding the baby while he pumped gas. He got done and walked up to the store, still carrying the baby. Came in the store, and that's when the woman, his wife, got out of the car.

Prosecutor: What happened when his wife got out of the car?

Joshua Harris: He was in the store back by the coffee machine, holding the baby in one arm and getting coffee with the other. I was up front by the register where I could see out the window, and I seen her get out of the car. I figured she was coming in the store after him, but she didn't. She turned in the other direction, like she was about to cross the street. About the time she got to the street, he came up to the register to pay for the coffee.

Prosecutor: Did he pay for the coffee, Mr. Harris?

Joshua Harris: No he didn't, because as soon as he seen the lady heading for the street, he dropped the coffee on the floor and took off running after her. I had one hell of a mess to clean up; I'll tell you that.

Prosecutor: He ran after Mrs. Lewinsky?

Joshua Harris: He sure did. Had the baby flopping in his arm while he ran, the poor kid. Caught her right before she got to the street.

Prosecutor: What did he do when he caught her?

Joshua Harris: He grabbed onto her arm and drug her back to the car.

Prosecutor: Did Mrs. Lewinsky go willingly?

Defense Attorney: Objection. Calls for speculation. The witness can't possibly know Mrs. Lewinsky's state of mind.

The Court: Sustained. Rephrase, Counselor.

Prosecutor: Could you see Mrs. Lewinsky's face, as Mr. Lewinsky led her back to the car?

Joshua Harris: I sure could.

Prosecutor: And what was she doing?

Joshua Harris: She was crying, and I don't mean just regular crying. She was crying that snot-running-all-over-your-face kind of crying.

Prosecutor: What did Mr. Lewinsky do when they reached the car?

Joshua Harris: He was talking to her and he opened the door and pushed her into the car. Then he put the baby somewhere in the back, and he drove away.

Prosecutor: No further questions, Your Honor.

The Court: Your witness, Mr. Stone.

Defense Attorney: Thank you, Your Honor. Good morning, Mr. Harris.

Joshua Harris: Morning.

Defense Attorney: Mr. Harris, were you inside the store when Mr. Lewinsky led his wife back to the car?

Joshua Harris: Yep. Glenda still wasn't back up front, so I couldn't leave.

Defense Attorney: So you witnessed these events through the front window of the store?

Joshua Harris: Sure did.

Defense Attorney: You stated that you saw Mrs. Lewinsky crying.

Joshua Harris: That's right.

Defense Attorney: Could you hear her crying, as well?

Joshua Harris: No. We keep the radio on inside the store, so we can't really hear much going on outside.

Defense Attorney: So even though you saw what appeared to be Mr. Lewinsky speaking to Mrs. Lewinsky, you couldn't hear anything Mr. Lewinsky might have been saying, is that correct?

Joshua Harris: That's right.

Defense Attorney: Is it possible he was comforting her?

Prosecutor: Objection. Now Mr. Stone is calling for speculation.

The Court: Sustained.

Defense Attorney: I'll rephrase the question. Mr. Harris, you have no idea what it was that Mr. Lewinsky said to his wife, correct?

Joshua Harris: That's correct.

Defense Attorney: No further questions.

Chapter 44
June 2-3, 2012

Mrs. Tyler stayed with us for nearly a month, and during that time Anna seemed to find her footing. No doubt the ability to sleep a full eight hours helped. Mrs. Tyler watched Peter during the day when I went to work, and for the short time his colic continued, she and I took turns walking him throughout the night.

Over time Anna became less withdrawn, losing some of the weight she'd gained and for the first time since Peter's birth, taking care with her personal hygiene. Instead of finding her disheveled and asleep in the stuffy darkness of our bedroom when I returned from work, I began to find her damp from a shower, sitting at the kitchen table and talking with her mother while Mrs. Tyler prepared our dinner.

True, I never saw her holding Peter, but that was easily explained away by reports of him napping, or even by my own eagerness to hold him at the end of a long day. When I was home Anna scarcely had a chance to hold Peter, so eager was I to hold my son.

If Mrs. Tyler worried over Anna's distance from Peter, she never expressed concern; in fact, she seemed buoyed by Anna's apparent return to normalcy. I, in turn, was full of gratitude for Mrs. Tyler, not only for her real and physical help during that time, but also for her quiet support of both me and Anna, and her obvious devotion to Peter.

As spring headed towards summer and the soybean fields around us began to sprout, oblivious to the coming drought that would render fields shriveled and burned by July, Anna finally began to show an interest in Peter. She held him sometimes in the evenings, alone in his room, rocking back and forth on the balls of her feet and humming a tuneless melody. As I peeked in from his open door and saw her gazing intently into his face, I wondered what she was seeing, what she was saying to him in those moments. Conveying her love? Pledging her protection?

How well she fooled us.

By the end of May Mrs. Tyler and I felt Anna was doing so well she broached the subject of returning home. Mr. Tyler had been unwavering in his support, but I knew he worried, not only because it was in his nature to worry, but also because he loved Anna, and Peter, beyond all reason. They were both eager, I think, for a return to routine, and witnessing the progress Anna had made I, too, was ready to have my family back, just the three of us.

So it was on a stifling Sunday morning, the heat index already edging into the nineties, that Mrs. Tyler packed her bags while Mr. Tyler sat at our breakfast bar enjoying a plate of sausage links, scrambled eggs, and toast prepared by none other than Anna. It was the first she'd cooked since Peter's birth, and it served to add to our belief that Anna was, if not fully mend-ed, at least well on her way.

Peter's colic seemed to have abated by then; he'd slept a full eight hours the previous night, waking that morning with a full diaper and an empty stomach. Now freshly changed, he lay in the crook of my arm noisily slurping down his second bottle of the day. Mrs. Tyler set her bags down by the bar and leaned over to kiss his head.

"I'll see you tomorrow, sweet boy," she said, then looked at me for confirmation. "Are y'all still coming for dinner tomorrow night?"

"Yes ma'am," I assured her. Although I had re-turned to work almost immediately after Peter was born, I had arranged to take the next couple of days off to stay with Anna. With Mrs. Tyler gone and me at work, Anna would bear sole responsibility for Pe-ter, and although she seemed to be in a much better place emotionally, all of us agreed it would be better to take things slowly. "I'm already looking forward to it."

"Good," she said. "And call me if you need anything before then. Okay?" She caught my eye, and I nodded.

"We will," I promised. "Thanks again for everything. I don't know how we would have made it without you."

She squeezed my arm. "Take care of them," she whispered against my ear as she nodded in Anna's direc-tion.

"I will," I promised, and I meant it, in spite of how it all turned out.

In just over twenty-four hours, Anna would be dead.

I awakened that night to the sound of Peter's crying, the first such night in over a week. Squinting, I checked the nightstand clock: It was just before three a.m. Anna stirred beside me. "Stay here," I told her. "I'll get him."

"No," she answered. "I'll do it. I need to get back into the swing of things."

I didn't argue, although those words would come back to haunt me. We'd spent a quiet day at home, but I was tired and we had a long drive ahead of us in the morning. Anna had suggested we take a day trip to Big Hill Pond Park, a beautiful park on the southern border we hadn't visited in years. I had worried it might be too difficult, particularly with a baby in tow, but she assured me not only was she up for the trip, she looked forward to being outdoors, hiking as we used to so often do. "I need some sun, Phil," she said. "Not to mention some exercise. We'll pack a lunch and take plenty of diapers for Peter and make a morning of it; what do you think?"

"I think I'll finally get a chance to use that backpack thing we bought," I said. "It'll be good for me. Like walking with weights." She smiled, and I wondered if she remembered our conversation thirteen years previous, when we'd taken a trip to Chattanooga to heal from the heartbreak of Anna's first miscarriage. I was feeling hopeful, I remember, looking forward to time with Anna and Peter, ridiculously excited to finally be the dad with the backpack. Anna had always found the outdoors to be healing; I saw her request as more proof that the worst of her depression was behind us.

I'd just managed to drift back into sleep when a second noise awakened me: the sound of running water, as if Anna were preparing a bath in the guest bathroom down the hall. I was curious, I remember, but not curious enough to leave the warm comfort of bed to investigate. Not until I heard Peter scream, a vocalization that was abruptly cut off by the sound of a large splash.

I jumped from bed and raced down the hallway, yelling Anna's name as I swung through the door and skidded to a stop on the wet tiles. Anna was kneeling, leaning over the side of the tub with her back to me. She turned her head as I spoke then stumbled back, holding a naked, sputtering Peter in her arms. "I slipped," she said. "I was trying to bathe him and I slipped, dropping him in the water." Her eyes were huge as she handed the baby to me. He was slimy with water, his skin freezing. I wrapped my arms around him as Anna handed me a towel and Peter regained his breath to release another shriek.

"He's okay now, aren't you little guy?" I wrapped us both in the towel, warming him against my bare chest. "He's so cold, Anna. Did you not check the temperature of the water?" I asked over Peter's cries.

"Of course I did," she said, her tone defensive as she reached to unstop the tub, the water swirling down the drain with a slurp. "What kind of mother do you think I am? He's fine; he's just scared. It scared me, too," she said, with a little hiccup of a sob.

"Come here, honey," I held out an arm. What a terrible experience, I thought, that the very day Anna pledges to move forward and reclaim her life such a scary accident would occur. "Are you okay?" She snuggled into my embrace, and I held them both until Peter's cries subsided.

"Why don't you go back to bed? I'll take care of Peter. I'd kind of like to rock him for a while to make sure he's okay."

She yawned. "I think I will. Thanks, babe." She kissed Peter's head. "Good night, Pumpkin. Sorry for scaring you. Good night, Phil." She stood on tiptoe to kiss my cheek before heading back down the hallway to our bedroom. I heard the soft latch of the door before I turned my attention once again to Peter.

"So how are you, little man? That was an unexpected baptism, wasn't it?" His head found its spot under my chin and I inhaled the scent of the baby shampoo I'd used earlier, during his evening bath.

She'd decided to bathe him, Anna had said, and I'd assumed he must have soiled his pajamas in some way, maybe a leaky diaper, or even more likely, a bit of spit-up formula. But his diaper and pajamas were on the floor at my feet, perfectly clean aside from showing signs of dampness from the cold water splashed from the tub.

"So why were you bathing him last night, anyway? And why in the big tub?" I asked Anna as she packed a diaper bag of supplies in preparation for our trip. I had made up my mind, as I tossed and turned the few remaining hours before being rescued by the alarm, not to ask Anna those questions. I knew no matter how casual I tried to make them seem, Anna would pick up on the unspoken accusation. Sure enough, as soon as the words escaped my lips, her shoulders tensed for a brief second before she turned to face me.

"Am I not allowed to bathe my own child?"

"Of course, honey. I just meant, it was so late, and I know you were tired. He seemed clean as a whistle. I'm just surprised you wanted to bathe him again, is all, especially in the big tub. He's a slippery little dude when he's wet."

"Look, Phil. I've put up with you and my mother for weeks, always watching over me, monitoring my every move, whispering about me behind my back. She's gone now, and you need to back off. Understand?"

"We care about you, Anna. We want to make sure you're okay. That's all."

"I'm fine, Phil. Better than I've felt in months, maybe years. Everything is crystal clear."

"What does that mean?" For some reason, her words chilled me.

"It means I know what I need to do. I understand the direction I need to take. You and my mother need to back off and let me take it. Now let me hold him while you load up the car. We are still going, aren't we?"

I was torn. A part of me wanted to call Mrs. Tyler, but I wasn't sure what I'd say. "Mrs. Tyler, I think I may have witnessed Anna trying to drown our baby last night." It sounded absurd, but more than that, I wasn't sure it was true. Things may have unfolded exactly as Anna said: She slipped, dropping Peter in the tub. That seemed to be a much more believable explanation than the one lurking in the back of my mind.

"We're still going. We'll need to stop for gas in Brownsville, but we should get to the park by ten o'clock at the latest. Sound good?"

"Sounds perfect," Anna said as she took Peter from my arms. Some instinctive part of me struggled with letting him go.

Chapter 45
June 3, 2012

It was a hellish trip to Big Hill Pond. There's no other way to describe it. Anna sat in silence the half-hour it took us to reach Brownsville. I, on the other hand, was plagued by what I'd seen, or at least by what I was fairly certain I'd seen. As much as I tried to tell myself Anna would never harm our son, the more I allowed myself to think of it, the more I was convinced she had.

It was the sound I couldn't deny, no matter how hard I tried. When I'd arrived in the bathroom, my heart pounding, my feet slipping on the tiles, for that split second before Anna turned and saw me I'd heard nothing other than the soft lapping of water against the sides of the tub.

No panicked alarm raised by Anna. No cries from Peter. No furious splashing as Anna struggled to regain her grip. Nothing except the quiet sound of water settling after previously being disturbed. It was only after I called her name that she reacted. She turned towards my voice and then stumbled backwards with a choking Peter in her grasp.

Dear God.

As I pulled up to the pump to fill the car with gas, I didn't even think about what I was doing before automatically removing Peter from his car seat and taking him with me. All the while, Anna sat immobile in the front seat, staring straight ahead. He was sleeping, barely even stirring as I held him against me with one hand and worked the gas pump with the other.

I took him with me when I entered the store to pay, holding him in the crook of my left arm while I poured a cup of coffee from the machines in the back of the store. It was when I approached the counter that I saw Anna exiting the car. At first I thought she must be coming to join me. Neither of us had slept well; maybe she needed coffee too, although that would have been unusual for her. Anna had always had a clumsy streak; she'd never wanted to take the chance of spilling hot coffee in the car.

But she didn't turn towards the store; instead, she headed to the street beyond. Throwing what I hoped was enough money on the counter to cover the gas, I ran after her, reaching her and grabbing her arm just as she stepped off the curb. "Anna? What are you doing?"

"Let me go," she said, and as she turned to face me I saw she was crying. "Do us all a favor, please, Phil. Let me go." Her voice was soft, clogged with tears.

"What are you talking about? Come here." I tried to pull her to me, but she held herself apart.

"I'm no good. Not for you; not for Peter."

"You're perfect for us," I said, leading her back to the car while struggling not to lose my grip on Peter, who had awakened and was beginning to cry. "Anna, what is all this?"

She didn't answer as I briefly released her to open the car door, then gently nudged her in. I soothed Peter before securing him in his seat and sliding behind the wheel. Anna was turned away from me, but I could hear her ragged breathing in the silence of the car.

"Please tell me what's wrong. Let me help you." I reached for her hand. She didn't resist; nor did she return my squeeze.

"You can't."

Behind us, a car honked an impatient reminder. I let go of Anna's hand long enough to pull away from the pump and get us back on the main road, then reached to take it again, holding it against my thigh in an effort to bring some warmth into her cold fingers. I was afraid, both for Peter and for Anna, but also for myself. "Talk to me."

"There's nothing to say. You should have let me go."

"Go where? This is crazy talk, Anna. You're not thinking clearly. We need to call the doctor again. We need to get you some help. Where were you going? What were you trying to do?"

"It's not what I was trying to do," she said, and her voice dropped so I had to strain to hear. "It's what I was trying not to do."

We pulled into the Big Hill Pond Visitor Center just before ten. Anna hadn't spoken for the rest of the trip, but at least she'd stopped crying. Looking back, I should have turned the car around in Brownsville and driven straight to the Tyler's home. Looking back further, given what had happened with Peter and the bathtub I should have called the doctor's emergency pager and insisted on getting Anna some immediate help. But how far should one look back? If I look back far enough, I see a marriage full of *should haves*, but isn't that the case with every life?

Isn't it?

I'm not sure why I continued on an obviously failed trip that morning. Maybe because I simply didn't know what else to do. At any rate Anna and I sat in silence for several moments before I opened the car door and stepped out to retrieve Peter from his car seat in the back.

"Bathroom break," I said to Anna as I straightened with Peter in my arms. "Are you coming?"

"No," she said. "I'm fine."

I nodded and turned toward the restrooms. I was halfway there when I heard the car door slam.

"Phil? Why are you taking Peter? Let me have him. I'm sure he needs changing by now."

I hesitated, which only served to annoy Anna.

"For heaven's sake, Phil, stop being ridiculous. You can't possibly relieve yourself while holding a baby. What exactly do you think I'm going to do? Look, I don't know what's gotten into you, but frankly, I find it insulting and I'm getting really tired of it." She approached me and reached for Peter. "Give him to me," she said, as she pulled him from my arms. "I'll just get his bag from the car and we'll meet you back here as soon as he's nice and dry." She bent down to kiss Peter's nose. "You need a bathroom break too, don't you sweetie? Phil, hand me your keys."

Still, I hesitated, but Anna turned to pop the trunk and retrieve Peter's diaper bag, and in the bright summer morning, the blue sky above, the sound of people talking and laughing, the smell of the lake, I felt as if we'd both been behaving ridiculously. We were both tired; we'd had a stressful few weeks. Maybe the day would work out after all, I thought. Maybe the fresh air would clear our heads and put everything back in perspective. I watched Anna sling the bag over her shoulder and slam the trunk lid before turning to continue my way to the restroom.

Of course, when I returned to the parking lot the car was gone, Peter and Anna nowhere to be seen.

Chapter 46
Ripley, Tennessee
March 5, 2013: Trial Transcript

Court Clerk: Please state your name for the record.

Amanda Whitburn: Amanda Lee Whitburn. People just call me Mandy.

Court Clerk: Spell your last name, please.

Amanda Whitburn: W-h-i-t-b-u-r-n.

The Court: Proceed, Mr. Young.

Prosecutor: Thank you, Your Honor. Okay, Ms. Whitburn. Where were you on the morning of June 3, 2012?

Amanda Whitburn: I was just past Dismal Swamp.

Prosecutor: As you can see by the chuckles, not everyone is familiar with Dismal Swamp. Where, exactly, is it?

Amanda Whitburn: Oh, I'm sorry! It's at Big Hill Pond, the state park over in Pocahontas.

Prosecutor: That's in McNairy County, right?

Amanda Whitburn: Yes, sir.

Prosecutor: So you were in a part of the park called Dismal Swamp?

Amanda Whitburn: Yes, sir.

Prosecutor: Can you give us an idea of what that particular section of the park is like?

Amanda Whitburn: Yes, sir. It really is a swamp, but it's not ugly like you might think. There's a boardwalk people use to cross over it, like a wooden bridge type thing. People go there to hike or camp or fish. It's really pretty, with all the wildlife and stuff.

Prosecutor: What time of day was it when you were at Dismal Swamp?

Amanda Whitburn: It was around ten in the morning when I started on the boardwalk. I remember because me and my fiancé camped overnight at the park, and I was mad at him because he wouldn't get up. I thought it was stupid to travel all that way to just sleep the day away, so I decided I'd go look around without him.

Prosecutor: So at close to ten o'clock the morning of June 3, 2012, you were on the boardwalk hiking across Dismal Swamp?

Amanda Whitburn: Yes, sir. I was heading towards the big tower, the observation tower they have there. They say you can see the whole park and even over into Mississippi from the top of it. I wanted to check it out for myself.

Prosecutor: How long were you on the boardwalk?

Amanda Whitburn: Not too long. It's not even a mile, so maybe fifteen minutes? I wasn't walking too fast.

Prosecutor: So by 10:15, you had crossed Dismal Swamp.

Amanda Whitburn: That's probably right.

Prosecutor: Could you see the tower from the end of Dismal Swamp?

Amanda Whitburn: No, sir. There's too many trees, and the tower is up a big hill, maybe a quarter mile away, as the crow flies, but the trail is longer than that because it doesn't go straight up.

Prosecutor: Do you remember what you heard that morning, after you'd crossed Dismal Swamp?

Amanda Whitburn: Yes, sir. After I crossed the swamp and started up the foot trail, I heard a bunch of yelling and screaming coming from up towards the tower.

Prosecutor: Could you see what was happening?

Amanda Whitburn: No, sir, not at first because of the hill and all. But I ran towards it. Everybody did. The screaming was terrible. It sounded like somebody was dying. Oh, sh—I mean, crap. Somebody really was. I'm sorry. I didn't mean any disrespect.

Prosecutor: That's all right, Ms. Whitburn. You say you ran towards the screaming. What did you see when you got there?

Amanda Whitburn: Well, I saw him and a woman on the tower.

Prosecutor: Let the record show the witness has pointed to the defendant, Phillip Lewinsky. Ms. Whitburn, when you say tower, you're referring to the observation tower at Big Hill Pond?

Amanda Whitburn: Yes, sir. They were all the way up at the top.

Prosecutor: Who do you mean by "they?"

Amanda Whitburn: Him. The … what do you call it? Defendant. And a lady.

Prosecutor: How tall is that tower?

Amanda Whitburn: They say it's seventy feet. You really haven't ever seen it? You should go see it some-time.

Prosecutor: I may just do that. So when you arrived at the tower you saw the defendant and Mrs. Lewinsky near the top. What were they doing?

Amanda Whitburn: They were yelling and screaming, and she … the lady, I mean … she was holding a baby by the arm over the fencing at the top of the tower. Like she was trying to hang onto it and keep it from falling.

Defense Attorney: Objection. The witness is speculating. It's just as likely the lady was trying to drop it.

The Court: Sustained. But Counselor, that was a pretty speculative comment you made, yourself. Watch it, now. The jury should disregard both comments. Continue with your witness, Mr. Young.

Prosecutor: Just describe exactly what you saw. Don't try to guess at anything.

Amanda Whitburn: Okay. Sorry. Anyway, she was hanging onto the baby's arm and leaning way over the fence, like she had climbed up it a little ways, and they were fighting. I couldn't make out what they were saying, exactly, because they were so high up, but they sounded mad. And then all of a sudden he—Mr. Lewinsky—gave the lady this big push and grabbed the baby, and she…she fell. It was awful. I knew she had to be dead, she hit the ground so hard. Then everybody started running toward her and screaming, and I called nine-one-one but it took a while to get through on account of how out of the way it all is.

Prosecutor: What was Mr. Lewinsky doing during this time?

Amanda Whitburn: He was still up on the tower, and it looked like he was hitting that little baby, like he was hitting him right in the stomach.

The Court: Order. We will have order in this courtroom, or Mr. Stone, your client will be removed.

Prosecutor: What happened next, Ms. Whitburn?

Amanda Whitburn: Well, the ambulance got there and they loaded her up on the stretcher, trying to work on her, you know, and the police came and ordered Mr. Lewinsky off the tower. They told him to hand over the baby, and he did. Then they cuffed him and put him in the car, and that was pretty much the end of it, except they roped off the whole tower and I never did get a chance to climb it.

Prosecutor: I have no further questions for this witness, Your Honor.

The Court: Mr. Stone? Your witness.

Defense Attorney: Good afternoon, Ms. Whitburn.

Amanda Whitburn: Good afternoon.

Defense Attorney: You testified that you couldn't hear exactly what the Lewinskys were saying because they were so far up the tower, is that correct?

Amanda Whitburn: Yes, sir.

Defense Attorney: And that you saw Mrs. Lewinsky holding the baby over the side of the tower by his arm, correct?

Amanda Whitburn: Yes, sir.

Defense Attorney: Isn't it possible she was attempting to drop the baby?

Amanda Whitburn: Oh, I don't think so. What sort of a mother would do that?

Defense Attorney: But you don't know that that wasn't the case, correct?

Amanda Whitburn: Well, I don't know for sure, but—

Defense Attorney: You also testified that Mr. Lewinsky appeared to be hitting the baby in the stomach, correct?

Amanda Whitburn: Yes, sir.

Defense Attorney: But could you actually see the baby's stomach from your position on the ground?

Amanda Whitburn: Well, no, because I was looking up from under them, but—

Defense Attorney: Could you see Mr. Lewinsky's hand?

Amanda Whitburn: No, not … not specifically, but he was raising his arm up and down—

Defense Attorney: Raising his arm up and down as if perhaps he were performing CPR on the baby?

Amanda Whitburn: Well, I don't know …

Defense Attorney: But it is possible, isn't it?

Amanda Whitburn: I suppose it is.

Defense Attorney: Thank you, Ms. Whitburn. No further questions, your honor.

The Court: Mr. Young?

Prosecutor: No further questions, Your Honor.

The Court: The witness may step down.

Chapter 47
June 3, 2012

I ran, which may seem strange to some, but I knew immediately there was no abduction, no stranger appearing out of the swamp who had absconded with my wife and son. I knew Anna had taken him, and I knew where she'd gone.

Always before on our trips to Big Hill Pond we'd parked in the lot on the south end near Travis McNatt Lake. From there, we'd hike less than a mile northwest to the observation tower before looping around to head southeast across the boardwalk at Dismal Swamp. We'd complete the loop with a short hike back to the car.

Anna had taken Peter to the tower; I knew it. It's difficult to judge distance in the park because the roads and trails are winding, but I estimated the south lot to be close to two miles from where I stood. I was a runner; I regularly went for long runs on the back-country roads of Lauderdale County. I could reach the lot in fourteen minutes—thirteen if I pushed my-self—less time than it would take me to find a park employee, explain the situation (I couldn't imagine *how* I'd explain it), and hope for a ride.

So, I ran, jumping over the young couple making out on Fox Hollow Trail, barely registering the shocked expressions of the elderly couple I shoved past on the rickety boardwalk leading to the access trail. I crashed through trees and wetlands when shortcuts were possible, finally nearly colliding with our car, which was parked haphazardly at the edge of the lot as if Anna couldn't be bothered to take the time to secure it in a space.

I sprinted farther, leaving the trail and slogging through brush to find the quickest route to the tower, finally cresting the hill and spotting her, the auburn of Anna's hair bright against the blue of the sky. I had always loved Anna's hair.

She was midway up the tower, holding the rail with one hand as she made her way up, and while I could not see Peter, I knew by Anna's awkward gait she held him against her with the other arm. Calling forth every ounce of strength and speed I could, I raced for the tower, fairly leaping up the stairs, yelling Anna's name, desperate to reach her before she reached the top.

I remember everything.

She reaches the observation deck when I have two flights left and turns to look at me. Maybe, I think, maybe she's going to wait for me. Maybe this whole morning has been just some crazy mistake brought on by sleep deprivation. She'll wait for me and we'll enjoy the view together, and in twenty years we'll laugh about how I thought ...

She swings one leg over the railing when I have one flight left.

I reach her just as she dangles Peter over the edge by his arm. Over the sound of my shouts and Anna's sobs, over the sound of the screams below and the wind rushing past my ears, I hear the *pop* of Peter's arm as he swings in the wind.

I leap for them both.

In the midst of that leap I manage to grasp Peter by the back of his jumper with my left hand.

And I manage to shove Anna away from him with my right.

I was pumped full of adrenaline, alternately terrified and angry, and I knew Anna was clumsy, had always been, but my goal that morning was not to hurt Anna; my goal was to save Peter. It's what Anna—*my* Anna—would have wanted me to do.

I hear the thud as she hits the ground, and the sound reverberates in the shattering of my heart. In the beat of silence that follows, I realize Peter isn't breathing. I turn away from Anna to tend to my son.

You told me to take care of him if you couldn't, Anna, my love. That's what I did. I kept my promise.

Chapter 48
Ripley, Tennessee
April 1, 2013: Attorney Consult

I was unable to read Brian's expression as the guards led me into the room and removed my cuffs. He waited until we were alone before coming to sit across from me.

"I have some good news, and some bad news," he said. "Which do you want first?"

"The good news," I replied. "I've had enough bad news lately to last a lifetime."

"Okay, then." He sat back, hands on his knees, and took a deep breath. "It seems you were right, and I was wrong."

"About?"

"About Peter."

My heart thudded in my chest. "What do you mean?"

He allowed himself the smallest of smiles. "There's been some improvement."

"I knew it!" I nearly leapt from my chair before Brian held out a restraining hand. "What's he doing? What do they see?"

"He's tracking objects with his eyes. At first they thought it was coincidence, so I didn't say anything. Didn't want to give you false hope. But it's real. I went by to see for myself. And Phil, it gets better. He's making eye contact. He looked right at me. He responded to my voice, moving his arms. The doctors say these are very hopeful signs."

"Thank God!" I said, taking a few seconds to compose myself. After such wonderful news, I couldn't imagine what could be bad, or at least not bad enough to erase the euphoria I felt at knowing my son was *still there*. "Brian, this is incredible. And we're so close, aren't we? You've managed to tear apart everything the prosecution has set forth, and now it's our turn. We've got the expert testimony, and my testimony—" I stopped as he put a hand on my arm.

"Phil. That's the good news. The bad news ..." he stood, walking behind me to put his hands on my shoulders. "The bad news is that the test results are back."

I stilled, the joy of a just a few seconds ago seeping away. I knew what test results he meant. I swallowed, preparing myself. "And?"

"And you're not his father."

I had known, or at least strongly suspected, that that would be the case. But even hearing the words, I didn't completely grasp what they meant.

"But I'm on the birth certificate," I said. "And I was the one caring for him. For Christ's sake, I'm the one who saved him. Tests mean nothing, Brian."

He moved back around to sit across from me. "Unfortunately they do, Phil."

I sat back in my chair, my mind racing. "All right. So now what? The Williams guy, he's divorced and at least ten years older than I am. There must be something he can sign, something absolving him from having to pay child support, or whatever he's afraid of. I don't want anything from him. I just want my son."

Brian ran a hand over his face before answering me. "He won't sign anything like that, Phil. He's fully prepared to seek custody of Peter. In fact, child welfare is completing a home study even as we speak in order to move Peter there."

"But my trial isn't over. He can't just take my son because I'm in here. And what about Cathy? And Mrs. Tyler? Why would they move Peter when he's been doing so well there?"

"It won't come as a surprise to you that Cathy's skipped town. We both knew she didn't have it in her to care for a baby, particularly not one with special needs. And Mrs. Tyler is in her seventies. Her health has steadily declined over the past year given all she's had to deal with. So those are factors in the decision to move Peter. But the main reason is because he has a biological father who wants custody of him. This is a blessing in some ways, Phil, because had Peter not had a biological relative able to care for him, he would have to be placed in foster care."

"I'm glad Peter will be in a safe place, but Brian, I still intend to get him back. Placement with Anna's coworker will be temporary."

"I'm afraid that's easier said than done. Robert Williams is proven to be the biological father. The biological mother is dead, and the man who was married to her sits in jail accused of her murder. Has been sitting in jail, I might add, for most of Peter's life."

"But we're going to win, and I'm going to get out. Right? I mean, that's almost a given at this point."

"Yes, we'll probably win. And you'll get out. But Peter will still be Dr. Williams' son. You'll get your freedom." He reached out and put a hand on my forearm. "But Phil, you won't get Peter. He's not yours to get."

Before I could respond pain sliced through my chest, crushing me, leaving me breathless. Through the blood rushing through my ears, I heard Brian's voice, panicked, summoning the guards before everything faded to black.

Chapter 49
April 7, 2013

Myocardial infarction, they said. A mild heart attack caused by coronary artery disease. "Not unusual for a man your age," the attending physician said. "You're lucky you're so physically fit," he continued, "or it might have been a lot worse. You a runner?"

"Used to be."

He smiled, not unkindly. "I suppose in your current circumstances, being known as a 'runner' could cause problems."

I hadn't felt physically well in quite some time, certainly not since my arrest. I'd had periods of breathlessness followed by a moment or two of dizziness, but had attributed the symptoms to a combination of stress, lack of exercise, and bad food. "All of which could be factors," the physician agreed. "I'll send you back with prescriptions to help lower your blood pressure and cholesterol. I'll also make some dietary and exercise recommendations, but given your situation, they might not be easy to implement."

Brian insisted the trial be postponed until I was discharged from the hospital and medically cleared to attend court the following week. I didn't care; after news of Peter, what difference did it make to me?

"There's the small matter of having a right to be there, but more importantly, I'll be calling you to testify right after I wrap up with Martha Dunn," Brian said on the day of my discharge. The guards waited just outside the open door, giving us our privacy. "She's good, Phil, and I think the information she's going to share with the court is a very accurate description of Anna's last months."

I was swallowed by a wave of loneliness, the sadness enveloping me like a dense fog. It had been nearly a year since Anna's death and I still missed her terribly. In my memory she was the beautiful, intelligent, witty woman I'd met the rainy Memphis morning she'd come sliding across the floor on her backside and figuratively bowled me over. In my nightmares she was something else entirely, but I had no control over those apparitions and I knew they weren't really my Anna.

"That wasn't really Anna, you know," Brian said, as if reading my thoughts. "That's how I've managed to press forward with this. I remind myself that the woman we're discussing in court wasn't our little Socrates."

"No, she wasn't, but you know what bothers me?" Brian raised his brows at my question, and I continued. "It bothers me that I don't know when she slipped away. When did Anna stop being Anna?"

Brian rubbed his chin. "I doubt there was a specific incident, but I could notice subtle changes over the years when I visited you guys. Obviously I didn't know the extent of the problem, but that was Anna. She never was one to confide, was she?"

I shook my head. "Sometimes I feel so weighted down with guilt, you know? I should have known. I should have listened more. But I did try, Brian. I knew Anna had a hard time sharing any sort of negative feelings, so I paid special attention. You know what the irony of it all is?"

"Tell me."

"All those years I tried to be so attuned to whatever she might have been feeling, whatever grief or sadness or loneliness she might have felt because of Jeffrey, or the miscarriages, or even our decision not to have children. I worked so hard to be sensitive to those issues, and in the end, that seems to be what destroyed her."

"What do you mean?"

I struggled to put it into words. "Williams, the guy ... Peter's father." I forced myself to say it, ripping off the scab I'd spent nearly two years creating. "He said Anna worried she wasn't enough for me. That I might prefer someone else, someone who could have children with me. There were a couple of times Anna became angry with me—furious, really, to the extent Anna ever became furious—when I mentioned not having had children. She accused me of not being able to let go of the past, said I was holding her back."

"Don't do this to yourself, Phil."

"All those years, all those assumptions about what Anna must be feeling, and I got it all so wrong."

"Don't you think Anna bears some of the blame for that? It takes two to create a misunderstanding, after all. At any given time, on any given day, Anna could have chosen to address the issues between the two of you, but she didn't. You can't shoulder the responsibility for the choices she made. Take the pregnancy, for example. What would you have done if she'd insisted on getting an abortion?"

I winced at the word. "What could I have done? I would have been sad, upset, even angry, but I wouldn't have left her. We would have had a rough time, but we'd have made it through. Even knowing all I know now, I think we would have made it. And even if we hadn't, at least she'd still be alive."

"But Peter wouldn't."

"No. Peter wouldn't. But Brian, would he have been better off, too? What quality of life can he possibly have now?"

"I don't think those are questions either of us can answer. I know I'm certainly not qualified to determine the quality of anyone else's life. Hell, I can't even figure out my own. And it's a moot point, anyway, because she didn't insist, did she?"

"No. Not after that first day. She never mentioned it again. She cancelled her appointment—at least I assume she did—without ever mentioning it to me."

"Look, Phil, my point isn't to say whether or not your decisions or Anna's decisions were the right ones. I can't do that. My point is that Anna made choices along the way, too, and you can't take responsibility for those."

"But she wasn't well, Brian. It was my job to take care of her, and I failed."

Brian regarded me for a moment before shaking his head. "You're not as powerful as you think you are, Phil. No matter how much you want to, you can't always keep everyone safe and make everything turn out okay. Anna was responsible for Anna. Don't forget that when I put you on the stand."

He turned to leave, patting one of the guards on the shoulder on his way out. A nurse entered with a wheelchair and the ever-vigilant guards marched beside us until I stood at the exit. We rode in silence the short distance back to the jail, which was fine with me. I was lost in memories of Anna.

Chapter 50
April 15, 3013

The trial continued, but I was detached from it all. I felt slow and heavy, my brain struggling to make sense of the proceedings around me. Brian called old friends and coworkers to the stand to attest to my character, the state of my marriage, and my adjustment to fatherhood. Some part of me recognized the irony of their testimony; they spoke of me in relation to my family, my friends, my job, but I had none of those things. Who, then, was I?

"Object Relations Theory," I heard Anna saying, and in my memory she was wearing a yellow sundress and chewing on a straw, one of those little stir-straws used for mixing sugar and cream with coffee. It was a Saturday morning, the summer after our graduation. We were sitting on the patio of a coffeehouse in downtown Memphis, full of ourselves and our observations.

We were confident back then; some may have said cocky. We had the world at our feet, and like all young college graduates we knew everything and loved nothing so much as discussing our profound insights with one another over coffee (on those mornings we felt particularly sophisticated), or booze (on those nights we were still young enough to think we needed to prove our membership into adulthood by the number of drinks we could handle).

"Uh-oh." Brian set his cup down and leaned back, hands clasped behind his head. "Socrates is getting ready to pontificate."

We, or rather Anna and Brian, had been discussing Brian's love life, a frequent topic in those days and an area of some contention. The apartment the three of us shared was small, and the parade of women Brian rotated through was large. Whereas I, and undoubtedly Brian, were most inconvenienced due to the fact we shared a room, Anna was troubled by Brian's apparent lack of real interest or affection for any of his obviously willing participants.

"But they're *people*, Brian," she had said that morning as she smeared grape jelly over a bagel in quick, jerky motions. This, I realized in the middle of my memory, was something I had always loved about Anna—her complete lack of pretension, her eschewing bean sprouts or tofu in favor of good old-fashioned grape jelly. But that morning she was agitated, I knew, not only by the situation, but by Brian's mocking dismissal of her concerns. "You can't just *use* them."

"That statement," Brian said, pointing at Anna while looking at me, "is an excellent example of sexism." He turned back to Anna. "What makes you think I'm using them? What if, in fact, they're using *me*? It's possible, you know. I mean, just *look* at this."

He gestured toward himself, his mouth quirked in a smile, his legs tanned and muscular in khaki shorts. "It's tiring, always fighting them off. Exhausting, I tell you."

Anna rolled her eyes. "I'm not saying they don't want to be there. Good God, that last one had her drawers halfway off before you even closed your door."

Brian laughed. "That may be a slight exaggeration," he said, "inappreciable, but still, let's stick to the facts." He ducked as Anna tossed the chewed straw in his direction.

"Object Relations Theory," she had pronounced then, and I slumped down in my chair, stretching my legs in front of me to prop my feet on the brackets under the table. It was a beautiful morning, the café awning providing just enough shade, the breeze ruffling Anna's yellow dress until she gathered the hem under her thighs and sat on it. I had that lazy, dissociated feeling that sometimes comes when one is completely at peace, utterly content in one's surroundings. I settled in to enjoy the debate.

"I'm not pontificating," Anna argued, "I'm trying to offer you some insight into your deviance."

"Okay, I'll bite, just for fun. What the hell are you talking about?"

"It's a theory; I don't remember who came up with it. Several people. British, I think. Anyway, the premise is that we define ourselves by our relationships to the objects around us. Or at least that's what I got out of it; it was a really hard class, with a really boring teacher. But that part stuck with me. The theory is pretty interesting, if you think about it."

"Explain."

I closed my eyes, enjoying the sun and the sound of Anna's voice as she continued. "Your ego, your *self*, only exists in relation to something else. Or someone else. Or, in your case, lots of someones."

"You're saying I don't exist without women?"

"Sort of. Your definition of who you are comes from your interactions with women. If the women were removed, who would you be?"

"I'm not quite that simple, Anna. I also have friends, a job, a family. Okay, the family leaves something to be desired, but you know what I mean."

"All of which are objects, according to the theory. Who are you without all that? You define yourself by your relationship with your mother, your relationships with women, your job performance. External stuff."

"But the same could be said about any of us, right? According to your theory, we're all just using each other to define who we are."

"True," Anna acknowledged, "but doesn't that give us some responsibility to not harm them in the process?"

Brian whistled. "I've got to hand it to you; that's deep stuff. Too deep for me this morning. But let me assure you, any moans or groans you hear coming from the bedroom aren't because I'm harming anyone."

"You're incorrigible," said Anna with a sigh. "But you know I'm right."

"No," said Brian, "I don't. But what I *do* know is that I have a whole weekend ahead of me. That's forty-eight hours to find more women to help give me a sense of self, and I'm sitting here wasting them. Whose turn is it to pay? I've got theories to research."

I sat up, reaching for my wallet as Anna leaned across the table to peer at Brian. "Who are you, lover boy, without all the women? Without all the *objects*?"

Her voice was light, teasing, but Brian stilled, his expression unexpectedly solemn, any hint of playfulness gone. "Who are any of us, Anna? If this so-called theory is right, wouldn't that mean our lives are nothing more than a reaction to whatever—or whomever—we choose to keep around us? If that's the case, we'd better be really careful with our choices, hadn't we?"

Who, indeed? Sitting at the defense table with Brian and an assortment of the best attorneys my assets could buy, I realized as my former friends and coworkers swore under oath I'd been an excellent father, a loving husband, a competent coworker, I was no one. My *objects*, as Anna would have said, no longer existed, and so neither did I. Perhaps, as Brian had said decades before, I had chosen unwisely. Or perhaps, and more likely, the most subtle variation, the most infinitesimal disparity, can inadvertently destroy the entire system.

Chapter 51
April 16, 2013

Martha Dunn, a psychologist from Memphis, testified for the better part of two days. Brian had consulted with several mental health experts, all of whom agreed that at the very least, Anna had suffered from a severe case of postpartum depression. Mrs. Dunn, a self-proclaimed expert in women's issues, believed Anna's suffering ran deeper than that, testifying in a strident manner, her voice loud and nasally, that according to her research Anna most likely suffered from postpartum psychosis, a diagnosis I'd never even heard of until the trial.

Mrs. Dunn told the jury that her review of Anna's doctors' notes, in conjunction with her interviews with both Cathy and Mrs. Tyler, led her to believe that Anna was not only severely depressed, but also delusional. "She vacillated between thinking the baby was evil," she testified, "and believing she—Mrs. Lewinsky herself—was evil. Sometimes she expressed a need to save the baby, and other times she expressed a need to save herself. According to the notes provided by her OBGYN, Anna felt both her husband and her mother were plotting against her, and at her most dysfunctional, she was convinced their actions were in some way influenced—directed, even— by the baby."

"What causes postpartum psychosis?" Brian asked. He paced in front of the witness box, hands clasped behind his back, ever the professional. In such moments he seemed a completely different person from the Brian who'd crashed at our house, feet propped on the coffee table, a beer in his hand.

"It's extremely rare," Mrs. Dunn was saying, "affecting only about one woman in a thousand, and while there is no definitive cause, fluctuating hormone levels are believed to be a contributing factor to postpartum depression. We know that women who have a history of mental illness, or who have a family history of mental illness, are then at greater risk of developing postpartum psychosis."

Brian gazed at the floor, as if gathering his thoughts. "Mrs. Lewinsky had a history of major depression after the death of her newborn son in 2001. Could this have placed her at a higher risk for developing postpartum depression or even postpartum psychosis after the birth of her second son?"

As the prosecuting attorney voiced his objection to Brian's question a soft cry rose in the courtroom, followed by rustling sounds and the quiet thump of the door. I knew without looking Mrs. Tyler had hurried from the room, unable to listen to more of Mrs. Dunn's testimony. I also knew she must have been wrestling with the same guilt I was feeling. Anna had been unwell, and we hadn't saved her.

Brian continued with a few more inquiries before the prosecuting attorney took his turn, clarifying through his questions and her responses that Mrs. Dunn had never met Anna and certainly couldn't attest to Anna's state of mind on the morning of her death.

"Were you there the morning of June 3, 2012, Mrs. Dunn?"

"No. I was not."

"Had you spoken to Mrs. Lewinsky that morning?"

"No. Of course not."

"So you can't speak to her state of mind that morning; is that correct?"

"I can't speak to her state of mind that particular morning, but from my interviews—"

"Thank you, Mrs. Dunn. No further questions."

Shortly thereafter the judge imparted some directions to the jury and we adjourned for the day, Brian standing with me as the guards prepared to transport me back to my cell. "You're up tomorrow, Phillip," he said. "I'll lead you through events just as we've discussed. Finally, it's your chance to help the jury understand what really happened. Try to get some rest tonight, okay? You'll need to be sharp tomorrow."

But as it turned out, I got no rest at all.

Chapter 52
April 16, 2013

Other than Brian and his team of attorneys, the only visitor I'd had during my months of incarceration had been my pastor, who showed up every week or two to pray with me. I never knew, during those fervent sessions, whether the prayers were for me or for him. He seemed to feel a great sense of responsibility for my soul, much more than I felt, and I imagined his impassioned pleas for God to save me as bullet points on a resume: *Pastor, 2002-2013, Built a new wing onto the church and saved ten souls.*

No doubt I'm being unfair; I suppose I should have been grateful for the company. After all, no one else had bothered to come, the circumstances too awkward and uncomfortable to navigate. Nevertheless, when the guard announced I had a visitor, my first inclination was to decline. I wanted to be left alone. I had neither the energy nor the interest in conversing with anyone, and I no longer cared to be saved.

"Not the preacher," the young guard said, leading me from my cell. "An old woman. I've seen her in court. Don't know who she is; they just told me to get you."

I hesitated when I saw her, suddenly afraid, not of what she might say or do, but of the emotions her presence brought to the surface. She didn't look up as I took my seat. I don't think she was aware I was there until I placed my hand on the glass. She lifted her head then, slowly, and even more slowly her hand, until she placed it on the glass opposite mine.

"Phillip."

"Mrs. Tyler."

She looked awful, pale and drawn, much older than she'd looked just a few short months ago, a husk of a woman. I had the eerie feeling she might crumble to dust in front of me.

"We've had a hard time, haven't we, Phil?"

I swallowed against the dryness in my throat before nodding.

She nodded back, as if I'd confirmed what she'd feared to be true, then lowered her hand and sat forward, her face close to the cutout in the partition. "I'm not supposed to be here, you know. They told me not to come. But who are they to tell me anything, really?"

She didn't seem to expect an answer, and I didn't offer one; I just waited.

Another nod, as if agreeing with an internal voice I couldn't hear, and then, "We tried, but not hard enough. No. Not hard enough."

"I wish—" I started, but she cut me off.

"No. Wishes won't get us anywhere." She sat quietly, seemingly lost in thought, before startling, as if remembering something. "They'll let me see Peter, so I do have that. He's my grandson; they can't take that away from me. That man, Mr. Williams. He said he wants me to stay as involved as I want to be."

Something hot and heavy moved inside my chest. "I'm glad," I said, the words not expressing even a fraction of what I felt.

"Tell me one thing, Phil," she said, leaning so close to the partition it fogged with her breath.

"Anything," I promised.

"Was there a chance, any chance at all, that maybe ..." She trailed off, looking down at her hands, twisting them in her lap.

"What?"

I saw her shoulders rise as she inhaled. She raised her head to look at me again, and I saw Anna in the haunted shadows of her eyes. "Could it have been an accident, Phil? Isn't it possible that she didn't mean to ... that she wasn't really going to ..." She wiped away a tear. "I just can't imagine my little girl ever willingly hurting her baby. Is it at all possible, even the slightest chance, that it was an accident?"

My mind skipped back to that awful morning: Peter's clean pajamas in a cold puddle of water, Anna dangling Peter over the fencing, the pop of his arm, her peaceful expression as she went over the rail. I looked at Mrs. Tyler, the broken woman across from me, and my decision was made.

"Yes," I told her. "Yes. It was an accident. Anna would never have hurt Peter."

I saw the mental shift as it happened, the disbelief, the longing, the acceptance, and I knew I'd done the right thing. It was a gift that cost me nothing to give.

Chapter 53
Ripley, Tennessee
April 17, 2013: Trial Transcript

Court Clerk: State your name for the record, please.

Phillip Lewinsky: Phillip Daniel Lewinsky.

Court Clerk: Spell your last name, please.

Phillip Lewinsky: L-e-w-i-n-s-k-y.

The Court: Your witness, Mr. Stone.

Defense Attorney: Good morning, Mr. Lewinsky.

Phillip Lewinsky: Good morning.

Defense Attorney: Mr. Lewinsky, when did you first realize your wife, Anna Lewinsky, was pregnant this last time?

Phillip Lewinsky: I don't remember the exact date, but it was sometime during the summer of 2011. But that doesn't matter.

Defense Attorney: Excuse me?

Phillip Lewinsky: None of it matters now. It was an accident.

Defense Attorney: Yes, but we'll get to that. Let's go through some of the events leading up to the accident. Now, once—

Phillip Lewinsky: No, I don't mean that. I mean Anna hurting the baby. That was an accident.

Defense Attorney: Mr. Lewinsky, wait and let me ask the questions before you answer.

Phillip Lewinsky: Brian, I appreciate everything you've tried to do. I really do. But I need to let everyone know Anna would never have hurt Peter. She wouldn't have. I was sleep-deprived, not thinking right. I was confused. I thought I saw something I didn't, and I reacted in anger, shoving Anna—

Defense Attorney: Your Honor, I need to request a short recess to speak with my client.

The Court: Fifteen minutes, Counselor. We have a busy day ahead of us. We'll reconvene at nine-thirty sharp.

Chapter 54
April 17, 2013: Attorney Consult

"What the *hell* are you doing?" I'd never seen Brian so angry; I do believe, had the guards not been close by, he would have hit me.

"Finishing this. That's enough, Brian." I raised my hands in surrender. "No more. I meant what I said; I appreciate everything you've done, not just now, through all this, but always. You've been a good friend to me. The best."

"Phillip, we've got this. We're closing in on the finish line; it's almost over. You're *this close* to walking out of here." He held thumb and index finger a half-inch apart.

"To what?"

"Pardon me?"

"Walking out of here to what? There's nothing there."

He threw his hands up in frustration. "Look, it's been hell; I know that. You and Anna were dealt a shitty blow, a whole bunch of shitty blows. But you're still young, Phil. You can start over. I know it doesn't seem like it, but you can. You can meet someone else; hell, you can even have kids! You still have friends; you still have me. We can do this."

"No, Brian. I don't want to. The thought of 'starting over,' as you say, exhausts me."

"So … what? You plan on spending the next forty years of your life locked away in prison?" He gestured wildly about the room. "Or I guess you might get really lucky and they'll sentence you to death, Phil, because if they win, that's what they're going for."

"No. That's not my plan."

"Then *what?*" At Brian's raised voice, the guards moved towards us, but he waved them off.

"First, we need to change my plea. I can't continue with this … this *smearing* of Anna. It's like watching her die all over again every single day."

Brian took a deep breath. "I've told you from the very beginning in order for us to save you, you couldn't protect Anna."

"You did," I agreed. "And while I didn't like it, I had to do everything within my power to get out, to take care of Peter. But I don't have Peter now, do I? So we're smearing Anna's name for what? To prove my innocence? It's not worth it, Brian. Let's let her rest in peace. Let's give her mother some peace. There's nothing for me out there"—I inclined my head to the window and the bright spring sky beyond—"and there's no longer a reason for me to betray Anna. Let me change my plea."

Brian's expression softened. "Phil, it's not that simple. This is a capital case, remember? And the death penalty is a real possibility. We can't just waltz in there and change your plea. There are stipulations, regulations. For one thing, the evidence is pointing the other way. For another, I can't possibly argue that a guilty plea would be in your best interests. Look," he stepped toward me and put a hand on my shoulder. "I know how awful this has been for you. I can't even begin to imagine what the loss of Peter must feel like. But things will get better. You have to trust me. I'm going to go to the judge and ask for a continuance—"

"No."

"Be reasonable, Phil. A mistrial, then. Your little outburst in there surely prejudiced—"

"No. Let's just be done with it. Let the defense rest and move on."

"You don't think Young is going to have a field day with you in there?"

"I don't care. I'll tell him the same thing I was telling you. It was an accident. Anna was clumsy; she leaned over to take in the view and lost her grip. I was confused; I panicked. Or I was angry. Take your pick; it doesn't matter. The end result was that I shoved her."

Brian shook his head. "I can't let you go back in there, Phil."

"Then you're fired. Send in one of the other attorneys." I motioned him towards the door.

"You've lost your mind."

"Yes."

Brian paced, as he always did when agitated. "You can't do this, Phil. Please. Let me help you. I know you think it's all over, but it isn't."

"But it is. I'm not willing to destroy Anna's memory. Think about it, Brian. If Peter is lucky enough to recover, he'll someday learn about the trial.

And he'll discover what? That his mother tried to throw him off a tower? No. I won't have that. If he were still mine, if I had some influence, I could explain to him how much his mother loved him. But he's not, and I don't. He'll be at the mercy of tabloid reporters who care nothing of his feelings; they care only about selling a story. It will hurt him to know his father killed his mother, but it might destroy him to think his mother tried to kill him. Let me do this, Brian. For Peter."

I could see him struggling. He was a defense attorney. But more than that, he was my friend. Mine, and Anna's, too.

"I'll step back and let you and the rest of the team decide where to go from here," he finally said. "But don't fire me, Phil, because if you do, I can't visit you as freely as I have. At least allow me that."

"Of course. And Brian." I paused as he turned to look at me. "There's one more thing I need from you."

Chapter 55
Ripley, Tennessee
May 13, 2013: Sentencing

As I wait, I feel peaceful for the first time in months. There are many things I would change if I could go back in time, but at this point wallowing in my regrets is an exercise in futility. What's done is done, and I've tried to leave it the best I can. In the beginning I saved Peter, and in the end, I saved Anna.

The one I worry about is Brian.

"What was done with the equipment removed from my office?" I asked him the day I sealed my fate with the jury. "Where is it now?"

He looked surprised at my question, coming out of left field as it did. "It's in evidence, of course. Why do you ask?"

"Do you have access to it?"

"I suppose I do, if needed. Why?" A frown creased his forehead.

"What about the safe?"

His eyes widened. "No," he said.

"There was a man in Phoenix last year, a banker," I began, "who was found guilty of burning down his multi-million dollar home." I stopped as Brian stepped towards me, his fists clenched.

"Don't even say it, Phil. I mean it. Not another word."

"He collapsed in court, just after hearing the guilty verdict." I pressed on, trusting Brian wouldn't strike me. "He'd taken cyanide."

"Which was found during autopsy," said Brian. "This is a crazy thing to even be talking about. I'm leaving. I'll send the other attorneys in."

"But it wouldn't be found during my autopsy." Brian held up a hand as if to ward off my words, and turned to the door. "It would be assumed I had a heart attack. Look at my history. There would be no reason for a toxicology screen to be ordered. Two-hundred milligrams, even less, is all it would take."

Brian turned back to face me and I was struck by his appearance. He looked as if he'd aged ten years in as many minutes. All color had drained from his face and when he put up a hand to wipe sweat from his brow, I saw that it shook. "You can't be serious. Do you realize what you're asking?"

"I've got nothing, Brian. Nothing to live for, nothing to lose. One way or another, I'll get the job done. It would be better all the way around if it looks natural. You don't have to help me, but you can't stop it from happening."

"I'll report this to the guards," said Brian. "They'll put you on suicide watch."

"It won't do any good," I responded. "They can't keep me under surveillance forever."

"Phil, *why?*"

"Everything I cared about is gone. You say I can start over, but why would I even want to? Anna and I had a lot of good times in our years together, but we also had a lot of heartbreak. I don't want to go through that again with anyone."

"What makes you think it would be like that? Doesn't it ever occur to you that things might be different with someone else?"

"But I don't want someone else. I want Anna."

Brian dug his palms into his eye sockets. "I don't know what to say to you." He lowered his hands and I was surprised to see tears. In all the years we'd known each other and through all the changes we'd weathered in the twenty-plus years of our friendship, I'd never seen Brian cry.

"You say you've lost everyone you cared about," he said, his voice rough. "I lost them, too. I know it isn't the same, couldn't be the same. But you and Anna were the closest I've ever come to having a real family." He stopped, and I watched his throat work as he swallowed. "Has it ever occurred to you," he said through gritted teeth, "have you ever once thought maybe it wasn't Anna I stuck around for?" He slammed through the door and left me staring after him, stunned.

I haven't seen Brian since that day. He wasn't with the other attorneys at the table as I underwent cross-examination and court was adjourned. He was absent during closing arguments the following week, and again two days later when the verdict was read. I was found guilty, of course, which is as it should be.

I hear the jingling of keys and stand to be cuffed for my final trip to the courthouse. The cuffs won't be removed for the courtroom this time, the need to present as innocent until proven guilty no longer a concern.

The trip is quick, the guards quiet, and I sit alone with my thoughts. I miss Peter terribly, even though I only knew him for the briefest of moments. I haven't heard anything of him in weeks. I understand and accept he isn't mine; I suppose I always knew it in some still, small place in my heart, but I still love him as if he were. I know that removing myself is the best thing I can do for him.

I miss Anna, too. She feels very close to me this morning, almost close enough to hold her hand across the seat. My hand reflexively closes, forming itself around the shape of hers I still feel in my memory.

I was raised in the church; Anna and I attended regularly on Sunday mornings, and although I'm not completely clear on some of the details, I do believe in some sort of afterlife. I believe, too, that Anna and I will spend it together, whether in heaven, hell, or some other place entirely, a place set aside for people who make terrible mistakes based on the best of intentions.

The hallway seems dim after the brightness of the sunny day, and it takes my eyes a moment to adjust before I see Brian waiting at the door to the courtroom. He looks terrible. He's lost weight; his suit coat hangs limply from shoulders that are no longer broad, his cheeks are deeply creased, the downturned corners of his mouth nearly lost in the folds.

He grasps my cuffed hands in both of his and leans forward, wishing me luck in a voice loud enough for the guards to hear, then leans close. "Fidelity," he says softly, and then I feel it, the small hardness he presses into the palm of my hand, and I know that as always, Brian is there for me. My chest feels hot, my throat constricted, and for one brief second I lay my head against his shoulder. "Fealty," I return. I owe my friend so much.

I will wait until the very last minute, after the verdict is read and before I'm searched for my return to the jail. I'll wait until Brian is gone; I'll spare him the sight of it. After all he's done for me, I can surely do that much for him.

Book Club Discussion Starters

In the Prologue, Phillip begins telling us his story by saying, "By the end, even I knew I was a monster, not for the reasons they cited—not because I had killed my wife—but because I didn't save her sooner." What does he mean by this? Do you agree with his summation?

Phillip's father refers to Brian as a "man's man," and Phillip states he understands exactly what his father means, because he knows in his father's opinion, he's not. What do you think Phillip's father means? Why would Phillip not fit the stereotype?

At one point Phillip states that Anna's "Zen-like peacefulness" was something he initially admired, but ultimately hated. Why does he feel this way?

Anna frequently discusses Cathy's cruelty. Is this because she's afraid Cathy will do something to hurt her family, or because Anna is afraid she, too, might have the potential to become cruel?

Phillip states openly that he chose denial as a coping mechanism. How did this ultimately contribute to the destruction of his family? Had he been honest with Anna and himself, might things have turned out differently?

At one point, Brian tells Phillip, "You have your faults. You can be too rigid, too uptight, even a little self-centered." Do you agree with Brian's assessment of Phillip?

On one of their frequent camping trips, Brian poses the question, "Where do you see yourself in five years?" Anna responds, "That's a pointless question," explaining that life is impossible to map out so precisely because nothing is certain. Brian tells her she's pessimistic, but she disagrees. What do you think of Anna's points? Does she seem pessimistic, or simply realistic?

Several possible motives for Anna's actions towards Peter are discussed. She reports a family history of criminality. Mental illness is also discussed, as is postpartum depression and psychosis. What do you believe ultimately caused Anna's breakdown?

Phillip believes Anna knew she was unwell and tried to warn him. Do you agree? Should she/could she have done more?

When Phillip expresses guilt at not having helped Anna, Brian tells him Anna was responsible for her own decisions and that Phillip is not as "powerful" as he thinks he is. What does he mean by this?

Phillip's story concludes when Brian fulfills his final wish, having said to him, "Has it ever occurred to you, have you ever once thought maybe it wasn't Anna I stuck around for?" What is your interpretation of that statement? Does it change your perception of Brian?

More Books by Melinda Clayton

The Cedar Hollow Series:

Appalachian Justice, Cedar Hollow Series, Book 1

Return to Crutcher Mountain, Cedar Hollow Series, Book 2

Entangled Thorns, Cedar Hollow Series, Book 3

Shadow Days, Cedar Hollow Series, Book 4

Making Amends

Coming in 2016: *A Woman Misunderstood*, Tennessee Delta Series, Book 2

About the Author

Melinda Clayton is the author of *Appalachian Justice*, *Return to Crutcher Mountain*, *Entangled Thorns*, *Shadow Days*, *Blessed Are the Wholly Broken*, and *Making Amends*. Melinda has published numerous articles and short stories in various print and online magazines. In addition to writing, she has an Ed.D. in Special Education Administration and is a licensed psychotherapist in the states of Florida and Colorado.

You can keep up with Melinda on her website at www.melindaclayton.info.